Daniel F. Beatty

Ex-Mayor Daniel F. Beatty's Tour of the World

Daniel F. Beatty

Ex-Mayor Daniel F. Beatty's Tour of the World

ISBN/EAN: 9783337193997

Printed in Europe, USA, Canada, Australia, Japan

Cover: Foto ©Andreas Hilbeck / pixelio.de

More available books at **www.hansebooks.com**

☉ ☉ PREFACE. ☉ ☉

In 1878 we published a book (illustrated) of our

TOUR OF EUROPE,

embracing Ireland, England, France (Paris exhibition, 1878), Italy, Switzerland, Germany, Belgium and Scotland. We printed

TWO HUNDRED THOUSAND COPIES,

and have but one copy left, of this great edition. Some of the wood cuts are reproduced and used in this edition of our Tour of the World.

35,974 MILES.

In June, 1889, we again crossed the Atlantic to the Paris exhibition of 1889, returning last of August. So successful were these two European tours that we resolved to make a tour of the world, which we have successfully accomplished, traveling since last June, as below, 35,974 miles. A brief sketch of what we saw since last October will be found in the following pages.

Yours very truly,

DANIEL F. BEATTY,

WASHINGTON, NEW JERSEY, UNITED STATES OF AMERICA.

DISTANCE TRAVELED.

June 26, 1889.

N. Y. to Liverpool, - -	3,232
Liverpool to London, - -	200
London to Paris, via Dover,	275
Paris to London, - -	275
London to Liverpool, -	200
Liverpool to New York,	3,232
To Washington, N.J., via Belvidere, N. J. - -	100
Washington, via Belvidere and Tappen to New York,	140
New York to Glasgow, -	3,011
Glasgow to London. via Edinburgh and Forth Bridge,	460
London to Sydney and Colombo via Aden - -	12,500
Palestine and Egypt, - -	710
Blue mountains and interior of Australia, - -	500
Sydney to Auckland, - -	1,281
Auckland to Honolulu, -	3,900
Honolulu to San Francisco,	2,100
San Francisco to Ogden,	833
Ogden to Denver, - -	772
Denver to Kansas City, -	654
Kansas City to Chicago,	488
Chicago to Phila. via Harpers Ferry, -	950
Philadelphia to New York, -	90
New York to Washington, N.J.	71
	35,974

Total, Thirty-five thousand, nine hundred and seventy-four miles.

MAP OF THE WORLD.

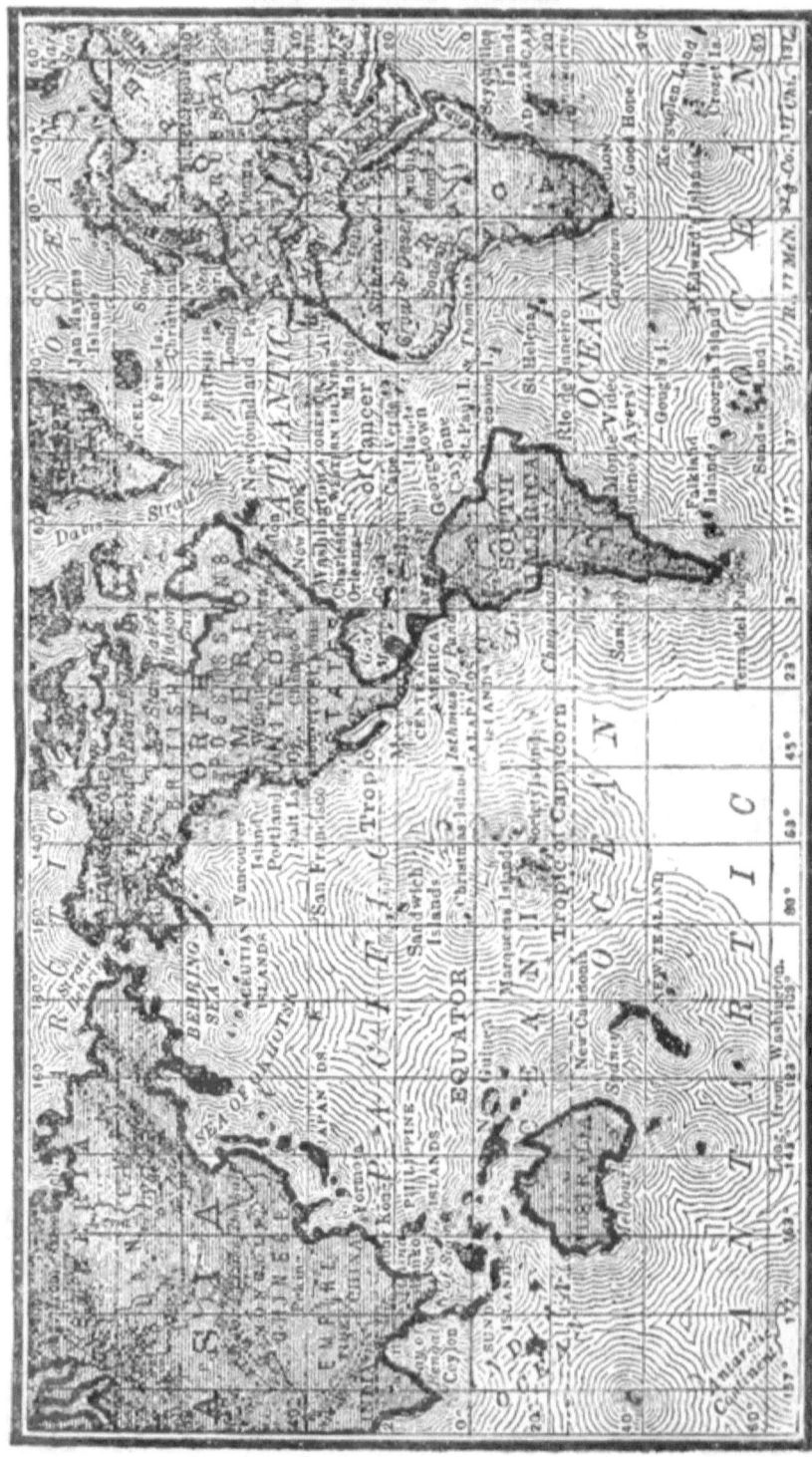

Yours very truly,

Daniel H Beatty

Washington New Jersey

BEATTY'S TOUR OF THE WORLD.

ON Friday, October 25, 1889, at 4.04 p. m., we step upon an express train for the great metropolis of America, New York. Here we find, at pier 41, many friends, who have come to bid us good-bye and *bon voyage* and safe return

FIFTH AVENUE HOTEL, NEW YORK.

to the United States. Saturday, October 26, at 7 a. m. promptly, the officers of the big steamer cry "all ashore that are going ashore," and we immediately steam slowly down the New York Harbor for a tour around the world. Near Sandy Hook is anchored the "Umbria," of the Cunard Line, and a French liner bound for Havre. Because it is so fogy, they dare not take the risk of going to sea for fear of getting grounded, but our pilot and captain take the risk, and before the fog lifts we are many miles on the great Atlantic, before the others are across the "bar." We find old mother ocean delightfully smooth, our ship is simply magnificent, table and staterooms all that one could desire, and officers all so kind and obliging. Sunday, October 27.—It is the ambition of a lifetime to visit the Holy Land, to see with my own eyes the spots made dear by sacred blood, where King Solomon's Temple once stood, Mount Sinai, also the great Pyramids of Egypt, the River Nile, etc. In a few weeks we shall be in Palestine (landing at Joppa—Jonah, 1-3—where Jonah embarked ages ago. "And he went down to Joppa." Here it was where "the Lord had prepared a 'great fish' to swallow up Jonah, and Jonah was in the belly of the fish three days and three nights" —Jonah, 1-17) and at so favorable a time, too, for the Rev. T.

JOPPA, PALESTINE.

De Witt Talmage, D.D., LL.D., of Brooklyn, New York, is expected to arrive there at the same time. No one more familiar with the Bible history is to be found anywhere.

OUR OCEAN STEAMER AT SEA.

Never before have we crossed the Atlantic and found it so friendly—no storms and but very little sea. The chief officer informs us this morning that he never saw the like at this season of the year. Now we are nearing the coast of Ireland; we have letters that we promised to write to America, so, kind reader, excuse us for a few moments, while we write and prepare the following cablegram: "Glasgow, Scotland, Nov. 6, 1889—Beatty, Washington, New Jersey, Advertise, Cairo, Alert, London." This cablegram code, when translated, reads as follows: "Advertise, arrived well, pleasant passage, address letters to Cairo, Egypt. Alert.—If you wish to communicate with us by cablegram, do so immediately, care New York Herald Office, London, England."

MOVILLE, IRELAND.

It is now 5 p. m., November 5, and for the first time since we started a signal is given to the engineer to stop. Here we are near Moville, Ireland. It is at this place the "Anchor Line" land all their passengers for "Old Ireland,' via Moville and Londonderry. A tender is sent out to meet them. This, however, is done before many minutes, and away we go for Greenock, Scotland, where we arrive next morning at seven o'clock. Here passengers who prefer may take the train for Glasgow, but no one does so, excepting the purser, as the morning is delightful for sight seeing on the famous river Clyde, one of the most beautiful and picturesque rivers in all Europe. Here on the banks of the Clyde were built the "Umbria," "City of Paris," "City of New York," and many other "ocean greyhounds." A gentleman who has resided in Glasgow for the last fifty years informs us this morning that never before in his life has he seen the Clyde and its shores to a "better advantage," so clear is the atmosphere. From Greenock all the way to Glasgow we counted eighty-seven large steamships being built; on both sides of the river were passenger trains, going to and from Glasgow. It was a magnifi-

cent sight, never to be forgotten. We have sailed
up the Hudson for 150 miles, gone down the river

KISSING THE BLARNEY STONE.

Rhine nearly 100 miles, but must say that the
scenery on the Clyde is quite as fine as either.
At last we arrive at

GLASGOW, SCOTLAND,

a city of nearly one million human beings. Our
luggage being examined by a custom-house officer, we engage a carriage for three shillings (cost
about three dollars in New York), call at the tele-

graph office, send our cablegrams, post our letters, and off to the railroad station for Edinburgh, fifty miles away, for there is no need tarrying at Glasgow, as we were here eleven years ago—1878—Glasgow being visited and fully described by us then (see Beatty's Tour in Europe). The route

VIEW OF GLASGOW, SCOTLAND.

from Glasgow to Edinburgh is full of interest. In the distance is seen the ruins of an old castle occupied by Scottish kings centuries ago, and a glimpse of the great Forth bridge is pointed out to us, and before we are aware the guard shouts

"EDINBURGH," SCOTLAND.

It's only a few minutes before we are comfortably situated at a good hotel just opposite

SCOTT'S MONUMENT.

After partaking of a hearty meal we walk to the Nelson monument and the old castle. From either we get a magnificent bird's-eye view of the city. All we have to say is Edinburgh must be seen to be fully appreciated. The next morning

SCOTT'S MONUMENT. EDINBURGH.

the weather is still fine, and seats are engaged on top of a "six-in-hand" tally-ho, for a drive of some eighteen miles to the great Forth bridge and return. This bridge was begun in 1883, and it was said that the last spike was driven the day we were there. The weight of the iron and steel work is 54,000 tons, while there are 240,040 tons of solid masonry in the piers; 8,000,000 rivets hold this great bridge, which placed end to end would reach from Edinburgh to the shores of France, and the surface painted will cover an area of twenty acres. But it is not our intention to describe Scotland in our tour of the world; it has already been mentioned by us in former publications. We return to Edinburgh, where we take a train for

MELROSE, SCOTLAND.

Here we visit the famous old abbey, etc. After seeing all of interest here, we step upon an express train, soon arriving at Carlisle, for the speed of the

"SCOTT'S EXPRESS"

is so great, often going at the rate of seventy-five miles an hour. To be frank, we are extremely glad when the good-natured guard calls out

"CARLISLE," ENGLAND.

Here a night is comfortably spent at a good, "home-like" hotel. The next morning a visit is made to the Cathedral, the old Castle where "Mary Queen of Scots" was imprisoned, etc. Later, taking a train for Leeds, the railway winds through a hilly country, crossing many pretty ravines and brooks. Arriving at

LEEDS, ENGLAND,

a stroll about the city was made, and we were very much amused to see an ordinary street car pulled by a full-sized locomotive. Well, after seeing all worth seeing here, we return to the station, step upon the great

LONDON EXPRESS

flying past Sheffield, Nottingham, Leicester, Bedford, etc., and soon find ourselves in

LONDON, ENGLAND,

a city of over 5,000,000 inhabitants, as the express train only made two stops between Leeds and London, a distance of over 200 miles, often speeding through the country at the rate of twelve miles in eight and a half minutes; so we were informed by an engineer, who knows what he is talking about. Being anxious to hear from home,

THAMES. LONDON.

we were driven to the office of the London edition of the New York Herald, where we received the following cablegram from our manager in America, in answer to ours sent from Glasgow:

"Washington, Warren County, New Jersey, November 6, 1889—Beatty, New York Herald office London, 'Emerald.'" This cablegram, when translated, reads—"We are well and doing well, and there is no reason why you should return." Tired and weary we were driven to a hotel, and after a good night's rest arose refreshed just in time to see

THE LORD MAYOR'S SHOW.

The Lord Mayor's show is one of the great sights of London, and the London papers describe this year's as the best ever given. This great show occurs once a year and has been given for centuries. The next day being Sunday, of course we help make an audience of over 6,000 to hear the world renowned.

REV. C. H. SPURGEON

just before he left for his annual trip to the South of France, for his health, as the great divine cannot stand the celebrated London fogs. Monday, November 11, 1889, is fine for foggy London, so we hasten to the office of the "Peninsular and Oriental Steam Navigation Company," to arrange our passage East, for by this company's steamers we are to travel 12,500 miles, having arranged for first-class state rooms on three of their great ocean greyhounds, for we are to break our journey three times en route. Of course we cannot think of winding up the day till we have visited

BARNUM'S AT OLYMPIA.

It was his first performance in Europe, the 15,000 seats were quite full, show good, especially Kiralfy's Fall of Rome. Barnum was there, too. The steamer we had intended taking was full, so

MIDLAND GRAND HOTEL, LONDON.

we were obliged to wait two weeks for another; but in London, the modern Babylon, time flies. A ride on the "underground" to Whitechapel to see the spot where "Jack the Ripper" is kept busy butchering human beings without being found out. Thence to St. Paul's Cathedral, which was forty years in building; height to top of dome, 404 feet. Entering, one sees monuments to the "great," beautiful dome, big organ, etc. Way down in the crypt is the Duke of **Wellington's** funeral car, cost $65,000. Now out around St. Paul's churchyard near by, Lord Mayor's office, Royal Stock Exchange, on top of an omnibus down Ludgate Hill, through the Strand, passing the Court of Chancery to Trafalgar Square. Here is Nelson's column flanked by huge lions; beyond, to our right, the **National Picture Gallery**, through Pall Mall (side trip here to Regent and Bond streets), pass St. James' Palace, the Prince of Wales' residence, fronting on St. James' Park; beyond " Her Majesty, the Queen's Palace." Over the park we go to Westminster Abbey, the most interesting edifice in the Kingdom; so much to see here, monuments to kings and queens, inscriptions to great men and women, etc., makes one weary; cross the road to the House of Parliament, where we enter, for we know some of the members. Coming out set our watch by " Big Ben," the great clock in the tower, 345 feet high. On the Westminster Bridge we get a good view of water front of the " House." Now take my arm, reader, and let us stroll up High Holborn through Oxford street to Marble Arch, cost $400,000, through which we enter Hyde Park, 388 acres, cross Rotten Row, pass the Serpentine, enter Kensington Gardens to Albert Memorial, cost $700,000; opposite is Albert Hall, cost $1,000,-000, holds 9,000 people; the organ has five rows of keys, 130 stops and 10,000 pipes; orchestra accommodates 1,000 performers. Now, let's go by rail to " Tower of London," whose origin is lost in the mist of antiquity, see the $2,500,000 crown jewels; cross the London Bridge, by hansom to Regent's Park of 472 acres, to see the finest collection of wild animals in the world; "Madam's" wax works, British Museum; then take night train for Crystal Palace, cost $7,500,000 (the Handel Orchestra seats 5,000 persons), and see the greatest display of fireworks in the world. On we go to Windsor Castle and see her most gracious

Majesty the Queen of England, and by pleasure steamer on the River Thames to Hampton Court, Richmond, Barnes Bridge and Common, to Kew Gardens; now an early morning ramble to the great markets of London, to see how much it really takes to feed London, and you know the two weeks have gone so quick, haven't they? Ten a. m., on November 28, 1889, we are in the great London (Liverpool street) Railway Station. Yonder is backing up a special train. "Where is that train going?" "Going!" exclaimed the guard, "that is the special train that is to convey you to your steamer, the

ROHILLA OF THE P. & O.

Who is singing in the waiting room? Why, it's a lot of missionaries bound for China and Japan. While they are bidding friends a long farewell, perhaps forever, they do so with song, ending with "Praise God from whom all blessings flow." There stands the famous Bradlaugh, a member of Parliament, for India; by his side is Postmaster-General O'Brien, of Singapore; there, too, is Mr. Legh, another Member of Parliament, and his charming wife, for sunny Egypt. Yonder, just getting into the train, are the Countess of Strathmore and her two daughters, the Ladies Lyon; near by Mr. Jessup and his man servant, of Philadelphia, Pa.; a good-natured captain and Dr. Rathbon, an American dentist, going to Gibraltar; an ex-mayor from the United States, member of the Chinese embassy and native servant, and hundreds of others bound for all parts of the world. Listen—click—the guard has locked us in our compartment, and away we go, through the city of London to the Royal Albert Docks. Thursday, November 28, at 2 p. m., they cry "all ashore that are going ashore," and amid the waving of handkerchiefs, hats, etc., we soon begin to steam slowly out of the

ROYAL ALBERT DOCKS

into the river Thames. Hark! there is a band of music serenading us as we leave the dock, for on all the P. & O. Australian boats a band of music goes all the way, 12,500 miles. We are now in the world-renowned river Thames. Leaving Gravesend, the great ocean greyhound begins to thread her way westward through the intricate channels that extend from the mouth of the river Thames towards the borders or coasts of Belgium and France on one side and "Merry Old England" on the other, to the Straits of Dover, where

WAGON ROAD OF NAPOLEON.

she enters the broader waters of the famous English Channel. On either side are millions of human beings, each country speaking a different language, simply separated by these waters. As we steam onward, the Channel presents a constant, moving panorama of steamers, moving inward and outward, bound to and from all nations of the earth. What a magnificent sight; Now comes Southend, the great "Nore Lighthouse," mouth of River Medway, etc. Finally, after a run of seventy-two miles, the heights, castle and town of Dover is sighted. On we go, passing

Beachy Head, Brighton, the Long Branch of England, on our right, and on our left Calais, and further on Havre, France. Soon the famous Isle of Wight is sighted, the summer residence of Her Gracious Majesty, the Queen of England. Here we stop to let off the Cnannel pilot. Now, leaving the English coast and Plymouth to our right, the steamer passes St. Catherine's Point, France, 197 miles from London. Soon we reach the

BAY OF BISCAY,

a body of water, it is said, that has no bottom, whose waters, sailors claim, go through the earth into the Pacific—how true this is we are unable to say. After passing safely over the Bay without going through, the first land we see is Cape Finisterre. All along is seen now and then a peep of the coasts of France, Spain and Portugal, as we

[THE CHAMPS ELYSEES. PARIS.

steam southward. With our field glasses we can see a bit of Virgo, Oporto and Lisbon. At Lisbon to-day, December 2d, the late Emperor of Brazil arrived via Cape St. Vincent; after rounding this famous old Cape with her historical recollection , the good ship enters the Bay of Cadiz, and passing Cape Trafalgar and the Pillar of Hercules, one in Spain, the other Africa, we soon arrive at

GIBRALTAR, SPAIN,

1,358 miles (by the route taken by our captain) from London. On the arrival in the Bay the following telegram was read:

"London, December 2, 1889.—The late Emperor of Brazil, with his family, arrived at Cape St. Vincent in good health and proceeded to Lisbon. Mysterious epidemic has appeared in St. Petersburg (Grip). $15,000,000 worth of property destroyed in Lynn, Mass." Now some one says there was a great fire in Boston, too. I wonder what has gotten the matter with America. Landing at Gibraltar I was very much amused to see men in the principal streets milking goats, and a big boy driving a wee bit of donkey to market.

GIBRALTAR, SPAIN.

We paid a visit to the Governor's residence, the old Castle, Cathedral, looked at Gibraltar's mighty guns, and her strong fortifications, taking a stroll through the beautiful garden, etc., of this famous old town of some 20,000 inhabitants. Directly opposite is Algeciras, where the Spanish have their bull fights. Looking south we see Morocco, Africa. The transformation scene from Spain to Africa is great, people are so different in looks and manners; while one race live in Europe, the other in Africa. Can it be possible? is this Africa, the "dark continent" where Gordon, Emin Pasha, Stanley and others have explored? how many have gone there never to return! We will never forget our first sight of Africa, the impression made upon us is lasting. Leaving Gibraltar, to our right still is Morocco, Africa, whose sultan's yearly revenue is $2,500,000, for his authority is supreme in spiritual and temporal matters.

To our left is seen Spain, with her millions of human beings, back of us the high rocks of Gibraltar towering towards the heavens; here and there is seen a mighty gun peeping at us as we enter the

MEDITERRANEAN SEA,

which is described as a "tideless sea." At Gibraltar the currents have been very carefully examined, and it is found that in the middle of the straits there is always an easterly current running

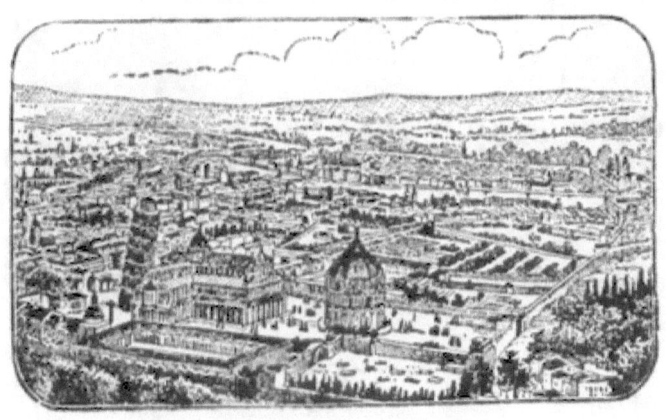

PISA AND THE LEANING TOWER,

in from the Atlantic at the tremendous rate of four to five knots an hour. The Nile and other rivers flow into it, but we are told it has no outlet. Does the water evaporate, or has it some unknown subterranean outlet? Who knows? Perhaps Vesuvius, Stromboli, or Mt. Etna could tell us; they may require this vast body of water to cool them. The great Sierra Nevada mountains having been passed by moonlight, we suddenly plunge as it were in the

GULF OF LYONS.

"The nastiest sheet of water on the globe." A fellow passenger who has traveled around the world three times, says this gulf has eight different currents. If he had said eighty we would have believed him, it was so bad, and to make it still more depressing, we had a

BURIAL AT SEA.

The ship is stopped, a short service is read; the body, wrapped in a white winding sheet, is slowly lowered on a plank down the outside of the ship. A gentle pull at the head and the body slips into the deep blue sea and disappears at once, as it is

VIEW OF ROME.

leaded or weighted at the feet. The signal is given and the ship moves on, leaving the fate of the departed to the sharks. It is quick and not expensive. Now we are passing near the coast of Sardinia on our journey of the world. December 7th, at 8 a. m., finds us only 150 miles from Naples. The sky is clear as crystal and blue as indigo; the atmosphere is perfect, for it is one of the Mediterranean mornings that we have read about. Yonder is Mt. Etna, and the Captain says it is nearly 100 miles away; we can scarcely believe him.

ISCHIA, ITALY,

is now passed, where only a few years ago an earthquake occurred, and 1,500 persons perished in "a twinkling of an eye." See, over there is the Castle of Elmo. Now we see Puteoli or Pozznoli; the place where St. Paul landed on his way to Rome. Acts xxviii., 13, "came the next day to Puteoli;" and as we are steaming up the

BAY OF NAPLES

Mt. Vesuvius is seen pouring forth hot lava and smoke. On either side the shore is dotted by residences and beautiful Italian scenery. Having visited Naples, the largest population 463,172,

POMPEII AND MOUNT VESUVIUS.

Rome, the capital, Florence, Venice, city of boats, Milan, Turin, Genoa, Columbus' birthplace, Pisa and leaning tower, etc., in 1878. Anchoring in

the Bay of Naples reminds us of former days. At
Naples we find the same hotel, same familiar
faces, and the Italian hackmen. Having already
climbed to the top of Vesuvius, gone over the ruins
of Pompeii, no need of our tarrying. At 11:30
p. m., the great anchor is lifted, away we go, and
soon find ourselves again on the sea. The following day is Sunday; of course the captain reads
the service of the

CHURCH OF ENGLAND.

On our return on deck we get a fine

VIEW OF STROMBOLI.

We are passing close to this volcanic mountain,
it is always burning. The town of Stromboli—
7,000 inhabitants—lies close at her feet; "seems
very risky." Now passing through the Straits
of Messina, to our right is Sicily with Mt. Etna
10,900 feet above the level of the sea, smoking.
To the left is the coast of Italy; either side is
dotted with villages, beautiful viaducts, trains of
cars, forests of olive trees. The hill country in
the distance looks volcanic, and beyond the great
mountains are seen covered with snow. Onward
we go, and it is not long before we see

CANDIA OR CRETE,

some of whose mountains are 8,100 feet high. Here
it was St. Paul sailed "close by" a prisoner on
his way to Rome. Acts xxvii., 13: "They sailed
close by Crete." Way beyond to our left is Athens,
Greece; to our right

MALTA OR MELITA,

where St. Paul was shipwrecked. Acts xxviii.
1, "and when they were escaped, then they
knew that the island was called Melita," In
Malta one can ·buy the finest laces to be had
in the world. We were shown lace handkerchiefs
for 75 cents that sell in New York for $7 each.
What a sudden change! Yesterday it was cold,
overcoats and warm wraps were in great demand;

to-day they are "not wanted." In the saloon the
stewards are busy putting up the punkahs, huge
fans just over our heads above the tables, and
little native Indian boys are to keep them in
motion while we dine. If one wants summer in
December, let him sail towards the coast of Africa.
Captain Maurice de Horne, of the P. & O. steamer

ST. ELMO, MALTA, BY MOONLIGHT.
(Near here tradition says St. Paul was shipwrecked.)

"Rohilla," informs us this morning, December 9,
1889, that the measurements of the sea as found
in sacred Scriptures, Acts xxvii. 28, are correct:
" and sounded and found it twenty fathoms, and
when they had gone a little further, they sounded
again and found it fifteen fathoms." Well, Alexandria, Egypt, is passed and we are near

DAMIETTA,

often fought over by the Crusaders. Here, too,
we see one of the mouths of the river Nile and
the great light-house towering toward the blue
Mediterranean sky.

"Only two hours more," and Port Said is sighted, 3,579 miles from London. As we approach to our left the coast of Asia to our right Africa, two great continents; we enter at once the Suez Canal, the great break-water walls extending far out into the sea. Soon the steamer is anchored in the Canal off Port Said, where she begins coaling, requiring 700 tons, while around the ship are hundreds of small boats filled with Arabs eagerly waiting to take us ashore, so much so that we are obliged to exclaim "yalla," "em

PORT SAID, **EGYPT, AFRICA.**

she," "go away," "clear out." Well, we finally went ashore, and, after passing the custom house, were soon very comfortably lodged at a good French hotel.

PORT SAID, EGYPT,

is in Africa, and is only separated from Asia by the Suez Canal. It is said to be the greatest coaling station in the world, 1,000,000 tons being supplied annually to passing steamers. Here one sees representatives of all nations of the earth. Rain falls in Egypt once in every three or four years, and it is a sandy desert excepting where the inundation of the Nile renders the country fertile. Port Said has no railroad, yet it is a town of 20,000. Approaching it from the sea, one is reminded of Long Branch, especially the frame houses. The natives, Arabs and Egyptians of the lower class, have been known to live on only a penny a day. Walking along the shore of Africa, we collected some rare shells; strolling through the streets we saw some very funny and amusing sights. Here we saw more professional beggars than anywhere else; "em she" was a good word to use to get rid of them. We are compelled to stop off at Port Said, for here we are to take a steamer for Jaffa, Palestine, for the

HOLY LAND.

JERUSALEM, VIEW FROM THE MOUNT OF OLIVES.

(Said to be taken from the place where Our Saviour stood when he wept over the city.)

Saturday, December 14, at 9 p. m., we embark on the steamer "Gironde," a French boat that arrived from Alexandria, "one of the finest steamers touching at Jaffa," arriving at Jaffa (110 miles from Port Said) early next morning; but we were unable to land, as the sea was exceedingly rough, and for five long, weary hours we laid anchored where Jonah embarked ages ago, and we pitched about at such a great rate, expecting every moment the Captain would give orders to proceed on to Beyrout. Looking toward the shore we could see the breakers often rising thirty feet. We had almost despaired of landing, when a fellow passenger exclaimed: "Look, see that boat; can it be possible they dare venture out in such a sea?" Well, these Jaffa boatmen are descendants of the Phœnicians, and it is said are the finest oarsmen in the world. If a boat is swamped each man will save a passenger, so if there are not more passengers than oarsmen you are perfectly safe. See, the boat is coming closer and closer, tossing about like a feather; it's floating the Turkish flag; it is the boat for the mail. The mail bags are thrown on board; presently the sea becomes a little more calm and a few passengers are thrown on board. Two strong men hold you over the rails of the ship, and as the mail boat comes up on a big wave, they "let go" while others grab you as you drop into the boat below, which an instant later has dropped below our steamer at least ten feet. Well, we were thrown in, too, and were landed "dry shod," but the boys demanded "bakshish," and they really deserved, it as they were brave men, and they got it. Now winding the steep streets of Jaffa for a little way we were soon in carriages and conveyed to a hotel, where we met Rev. T. De Witt Talmage's party, of Brooklyn, New York; on the hotel register the great divine had written: "Last night we made our exodus from Egypt, and this morning we entered 'Promised Land.' May our entrance to the Heavenly Canaan be as peaceful a disembarkation. We crossed the sea dry shod." Well, we crossed "dry shod" too,

JOPPA, PALESTINE.

Palestine is 140 miles long, by fifty to seventy broad; it's a hilly country. Joppa (now Jaffa), in Dan, is the port of Jerusalem and is certainly a

VIEWS IN PALESTINE.
(Nazareth, Mosque of Omar, Lake of Gallilee and Jews' Wailing Place.)

queer looking old town. Here is the house of "Simon the Tanner." Acts ix., 43. Here Jonah embarked ages ago and was swallowed by a great fish ; here, too, were the prettiest orange groves we had ever seen. But the people dress and look so strange, we did not know what to make of them. Of course we could address them "naharaside," "good morning, may your day be blessed," etc., and that's about all. Everywhere may be seen camels carrying their heavy burdens, frequently obstructing the highway. The natives still dress as they did in the time of "Abraham, Isaac and Jacob." We frequently see an old man in flowing robes, with long, white beard, who might be easily taken for one of the prophets. Desirous of getting to Jerusalem as soon as possible we engage six horses, two landaus, two coachmen and the well known dragoman, Mr. Rolla Floyd, who conducted the late General U. S. Grant, "Sunset" Cox, and many other distinguished Americans through Palestine, and at 2.30 p.m. are off for the Holy City (since we were there a rail road has been completed to Jerusalem). Now we are passing the spot where Peter raised Tabitha, as recorded in Acts ix., 36, "Now there was at Joppa." At 3 p. m. we drive upon the plain of Sharon (see Solomon's songs, second chapter. Soon we are beside the tomb marking the ground as recorded by Joshua xix., 3, "Hazer-Shual." "Well, I suppose you have heard of Sampson," said Mr. Floyd; "there is where he caught 300 foxes," as he pointed to an open field to our left. Judges xv., 4, "Sampson went and caught 300 foxes." On either side of the road on the plain of Sharon the natives are seen busy plowing in December. Tired and weary from the excitement of landing at Jaffa, etc., we are compelled to stop over night at

RAMLEH, ARIMATHAEA.

Ramleh is supposed to have been the home of

TOWER OF THE CRUSADERS, RAMLEH.

Joseph, who loaned his tomb for the burial of Christ. St. Luke xxiii, 50, 51. "All ready," cried Mr. Floyd, at 8 a. m. next morning, and we are on our way. Now, Gimzo is pointed out to us, II. Chronicles xxviii., 18., "The Philestines . . . and the south of Judea . . . Gimzo also; and the villages thereof." It is a beautiful, clear morning; little birds alight on the "only one" telegraph wire leading to Jerusalem, peeping at us, much as to say, "See, they are Americans." Over a little hill we go, and the town of Gezer is sighted, I. Kings ix., 16, 17, the town "Pharoah, King of Egypt, captured and given it for a present unto his daughter, who was one of Solomon's wives." "Please look over there on the top of that high mountain. Do you see that little notch or pass? Well," said Mr. Floyd. "That is the

PASS OF BETH-HORON.

There is where Joshua stood when he commanded the sun and moon to stand still. Joshua x. 12, "Sun stand thou still upon Gibeon, and thou moon in the valley of Ajalon." And we are told that the sun and moon obeyed, "for with God nothing shall be impossible," Luke i., 37. Looking toward this mountain from the valley of Ajalon reminds one of the Blue Mountains in America. Now, descending a little hill, the road winds more crookedly than the "Horse Shoe Bend" of Pennsylvania, but our horses are "quite used to it." On we go and Barree is sighted, a modern mud village, celebrated for its fleas. Soon we have reached

LATROME,

being half way from Jaffa to Jerusalem. Here, tradition says, was the home of the penitent thief who was crucified with Christ. "Lord, remember me when thou comest into thy Kingdom," St. Luke xxiii., 42. And strange to say the village unto this day is wholly inhabited by thieves. As we leave this town and are climbing the hills of Palestine shepherd boys are seen guarding their flocks, for in this country there are no fences. Arriving at Bal-elwad, we take lunch and have our horses fed, surrounded by the hills of Judea. As we leave the little stone hotel we find the hills barren, excepting now and then a grove of olive trees. "Look yonder, please, on top of that large hill; that is

KIRJATH-JEARIM,

where the Ark of the Lord rested twenty years."
I. Samuel vii., 1-2, "And it came to pass while
the ark abode in Kirjath-jearim, that the time was
long, for it was twenty years."

VIEWS IN PALESTINE.

Leaving the hills of Judea for a little while, we
now enter the lands of the

TRIBE OF BENJAMIN,

passing Abugosh, a modern village, at 1.10 p. m.
Here we see the ruins of an old Roman church, built
over 1,800 years ago. Way beyond to our left is

MIZPAH,

Here tradition says Saul was chosen King of Israel. I. Samuel, x., 24, " And Samuel said to all the people, " See ye him whom the Lord hath chosen." Descending another hill (for this country is very hilly), the road makes many sharp turns, winding around like a snake. To our left, tradition says, is the birthplace of

JOHN, THE BAPTIST.

St. Luke i., 39, "And went into the hill country." Here the late General Gordon resided a year. To our left is

EMMAUS,

where Jesus appeared to two of his disciples after he had arisen from the dead. Luke, xxiii., 13. "And behold two of them went that same day to a village called Emmaus." Soon we are in the

VALLEY OF ELAH,

where the " Philistines gathered together their armies to battle. ' Here is where David killed Goliath that the stone sunk into his forehead.' " I. Samuel xvii., 49. Here in the Valley of Elah we make another stop, for our horses are weary, warm and hungry. While the poor things are feeding we get a fine view of Emmaus. Hundreds of Camels are seen passing on their way from Jerusalem; by the way, the carriage road from Jaffa to Jerusalem and Bethlehem we found excellent; one need not stay away from Jerusalem and Bethlehem on this account; we wish we had as good roads in New Jersey. As we leave the valley, and are ascending another hill, the sights as recorded in I. Samuel xxv., 1-2, Isaiah vii., 3, also in Judges xx., 19, are sighted. In fact, all the country now is full of Bible history, for we are near Jerusalem, and just over there to our left is the

CONVENT OF THE CROSS,

said to be built on the spot where the tree grew that the Cross was made from. Nearly seventy-five miles away is seen Mt. Moab, near which were the cities of

SODOM AND GOMORRAH,

"And Lot dwelt in the mountain," Gen. xix., 30. Somewhere near this mountain, tradition says, was the Garden of Eden. "So God created man in His own image and put him in the Garden of Eden," first and second chapters.

VIEWS IN PALESTINE.

"Look here to your right," cried our excellent guide, "do you see that wall yonder? it is the old wall of Jerusalem," and sure enough, before one is aware he is upon

THE HOLY CITY,

so suddenly did you come upon Jerusalem, entering it as we did from Jaffa. We were soon in front of the Jaffa Gate, and all were politely

NEAR THE JAFFA GATE, JERUSALEM.

asked to "please get out of your carriage," for no carriages are allowed within the walls of Jerusalem, so narrow are her streets. We alighted, of course, and are soon very comfortably situated at a good hotel, built on

MT. ZION,

directly opposite King David's tower or palace. Immediately we order our Jerusalem guide, assisted by Mr. Floyd, to hire for us donkeys, as we want to go to the Mt. of Olives to get a bird's-eye view of Jerusalem and the surrounding country before sunset. No sooner said than done, for "here come your donkey, all ready," and away we go through the Jaffa Gate, not through the "eye of the needle," which is a very small gate within the large gate; turning to our right near the walls of the city, passing near by cave where tradition says Jeremiah wrote his lamentations. To the right, near the Damascus Gate, is where the stones were taken into a grotto and prepared for the Temple, so that there was neither hammer nor axe nor any tool of iron heard in the house while it was in building. I. King vi., 7. Here we go down into a little valley and again ascend a little hill, passing to our left General Gordon's site of Calvary; now descending another hill bearing to our right we get a splendid view of the

VALLEY OF JEHOSAPHAT.

Further on, near the Golden Gate, we are shown the spot where St. Stephen was stoned, and Paul, before he was converted, stood looking on. Acts xx.22. "I was also standing by." Down, down the valley our little donkeys take us without a murmur, as there is no carriage road to the Mount of Olives. On our right is now the Garden of Gethsemane; to our left, over the brook Kedron, are the tombs of the Virgin, St. Anne, St. Joseph and St. Joachim. All lie buried in the "Church of the Tomb of the Virgin." Now ascending the Mount of Olives, alongside of the

GARDEN OF GETHSEMANE,

that sacred spot. St. Matthew, xxvi., 36, "A

place called Gethsemane." Higher, higher up the Mount we go for nearly a mile, till we are at the very top of the

MOUNT OF OLIVES,

and we are amply repaid, for here the sight was

SIMPLY MAGNIFICENT.

as far as the eye could reach. In front of us is

MOUNT OF OLIVES.
(View from near the Garden of Gethsemane.)

the great yellowish-looking plain of Jordan, and we could see the river Jordan flowing into the

DEAD SEA,

which was visible for at least thirty miles, being some 3,000 feet below the level of Jerusalem. It was a large sheet of water of a very dark blue, but where the Jordan flows into it it was a much lighter blue. In sixty miles, as the crow flies, the Jordan's actual course measures 200 miles. Further on Mt. Moab, towering toward the heavens; a little to our right is Bethany; near is the "mountain" where Jesus was tempted by the devil. St. Matthew iv., 8. Further around is Bethlehem, Jesus' birthplace; still, directly under the setting sun, is a splendid bird's-eye view of Jerusalem, lying like a map before us; beyond, the Hills of Judea. No pen can describe the scenes. It was a view of the Holy Land that made the sights so interesting; the sky is cloudless and the sun is

RIVER JORDAN.

sinking in yonder western horizon, as it had done thousands of years ago, while our Jerusalem guide is pointing out the many Bible sites, where Jesus ascended to Heaven, where He taught the disciples " Our Father who art in Heaven," where He stood when He wept over Jerusalem. St. Luke xix., 41. " And when He had come near He beheld the city and wept over it." Further on, just beyond the Golden Gates, is where King Solomon's Temple once stood, but it has disappeared, vanished like the early dew. St. Matthew xxiv., 2, " There shall not be left here one stone upon another." Well, it's getting late and we descend the Mount, crossing the new carriage road to Jericho and Damascus. Now we are again in the Valley of Jehoshaphat; here we pause to see the monument Absalom had erected to himself 3,000 years ago, part of the monument being hewn out of the solid rock. Passing the fountain of the Virgin, the village

TOMB OF ABSALOM.

and pool of Siloam (St. John ix., 7) here a halt is made at the pool, to see hundreds of human beings, camels, horses and donkeys, who have come for a

cooling drink, etc. On the left of the pool, opposite
Jerusalem, on a side hill, is where Solomon kept his
700 wives and 300 concubines. I. Kings xi., 3: "And
he had seven hundred wives, princesses, and three
hundred concubines." This was a great many,
and the Holy Bible informs us that "his wives
turned away his heart." In front of us is the
valley of Hinnon, now the "field of blood,"
and the place where Judas hung himself
is sighted, St. Matthew xxvii., 5-8. Ascending
Mt. Zion, near the pool of Solomon beside David's
throne (near where we saw a group of Lepers) we,
enter again the Holy City through the Jaffa Gate
just in time to dine with the American Consul.
We were so pleased with our trip to the Mount
that we resolved to go again the next morning.
Tuesday December 17, was a beautiful, clear
morning, and an early tour was made to Calvary.
Ascending to the roof of our hotel on Mt. Zion we
were well repaid, for here we got another bird's-eye
view of the city; some one shouts, "Your donkeys
are outside waiting; come along, we must be going
before the sun is so hot." Again we are on our
way to the Mount, stopping in the Valley of
Jehosaphat to visit all the tombs in the "Church
of the Virgin. Now entering the real

GARDEN OF GETHSEMANE,

near by the brook Kedron, the keeper in charge
plucked from the garden olive leaves and ever-
lasting flowers for us to take to America. We
were standing on sacred ground. St. Mark xiv.,
34, "My soul is exceedingly sorrowful." No one
speaks in the Garden scarcely above a whisper.
With bowed, uncovered heads we departed, and
soon again were ascending the mount. We are
now standing on the rock that tradition says Jesus
ascended to Heaven from. Again we go to the
church of the Lord's Prayer. Here we see the
prayer printed in thirty-four different languages;
returning to Jerusalem via the Pool of Siloam,
King David's Throne. &c,. as before. At 1.30

p. m. we took carriage for Bethlehem, going by
the Pool of Solomon, near by where Solomon was
anointed King of Israel (I. Kings i., 38-39), over
the plain of Gihon, and soon are in the

VALLEY OF REPHAIM,

as mentioned in II. Samuel v., 18. Near here,
tradition informs us, is where the "wise men"
stopped on their way to Bethlehem, and "saw
His star" (St. Mathew ii., 2), that guided them to
where the Child was born. Near here we were
shown the stone that tradition says Elijah slept on
under a juniper tree (I. Kings xix., 5). Here we
get a fine view of Bethlehem and the surrounding
hill country. Now a shepherd's boy is seen watch-
ing his flock. Luke ii., 8, "Shepherds abiding
in the fields." Tradition says these fields are also
where Ruth gleaned (Ruth ii., 1-2). Stop, please,
this is the

TOMB OF RACHEL,

WAGON ROAD TO BETHLEHEM.

A little stone mosque has been built over the grave, as recorded in Gen. xxxv., 16-20. Beyond is the town of Zelah, where Saul and Jonathan, his son, are buried (II. Samuel xxi., 14). Here along this road Abraham must have traveled on his way from Berthel to Hebron (Gen., 13 chap.).

BETHLEHEM.

Now entering the environs of Bethlehem (Mich. v., 2), we see a beautiful grove of olive trees, the finest in all Palestine; no wonder, for we were near where Immanuel (Isaiah vii., 14) was born, in the land of Judea, for Bethlehem is built on one of the

VIEW IN BETHLEHEM.

hills of Judea. Soon we are driving through the streets. On either side are substantial stone buildings. Now we are entering a little tunnel built just under a residence; the streets are very narrow here, and will admit of but one carriage. Out into an open market or bazaar we go, and find we are in front of the

"CHURCH OF THE NATIVITY."

Entering, we were furnished with light and began our descent among the rocks and grottoes, into the stables. St. Luke ii., 7, "and laid Him in a manger." In Palestine it is the custom to build the stables under the dwellings now the same as in the time of Christ—"and Joseph went into the stable, because there was no room for them in the inn." Soon we were standing near by where "She brought forth her first born son." Men and women stood around, many reverently bowing low and kissing the manger, others are seen even removing their shoes. Not a word is uttered; it is an impressive scene. "Fear not; for, behold, I bring you good tidings of great joy, which shall be to all people" (St. Luke

PLACE WHERE JESUS WAS BORN.
(So says tradition).

ii., 10). "To all people" this is a glorious promise from "the angel of the Lord" (Luke ii., 9). Over the outside or top of the stables is the high altar of the Greek Patriarch, built directly over the manger, and where the inn once stood. Near here we enter another large corridor where we saw forty-four large alabaster pillars, brought here from the ruins of King Solomon's Temple. From here we visit the traditional grotto where the Virgin hid the young child from Herod, and afterward obeyed the great command: "Arise, take the young child and His mother and flee into Egypt" (St. Mathew ii., 13). Now, returning the sheik of the Bedouins with his escort gave us a treat to a sham battle on the plain of Rephaim on thoroughbred Arabian horses. They displayed wonderful horsemanship and great skill with their swords. Our dragoman (Mr. Floyd) joined them and rode quite as well. The sun was sinking as we entered Jerusalem.

Wednesday, December 18, again we visit

THE CHURCH OF THE HOLY SEPULCHRE.
Now we are standing on Calvary. "Look, please," said Mr. Floyd, as he lifted one side of the brass plate covering the rock that was rent, "see where the rock was rent." St. Matthew xxvii., 51, "And the earth did quake and the rock rent." Men and women were seen bowing low and kissing the very stone that covered Calvary. To our right is where the Virgin stood. St. John xix., 25, "Now there stood by the Cross of Jesus His mother." From Calvary we were shown down in the crypt to a grotto where the cross was found. Returning to the church near Calvary we enter the tomb of Joseph, where tradition says "they laid Him." St. John xix., 42, "For the sepulchre was nigh at hand." Here an aged woman was seen kneeling, kissing the tomb reverently, then, for a moment, she grasped the marble slab affectionately, with uplifted eyes. Now, armed with permission from the government, we are on our way to the

MOSQUE OF OMAR.

Soon we have passed near by the "Jews' Wailing Place," entering the grounds where once stood the Temple. Before going into the Mosque we are obliged to remove our shoes or cover them with slippers. At last we are in the Mosque where once stood

KING SOLOMON'S TEMPLE.

One could scarcely realize it. In front of us is the Holy Rock where Abraham offered his son Isaac for a sacrifice, which is fenced in so no "unclean hand" can touch it. This rock is supposed by many Mohammedans to be suspended in the air, and if touched by any "unclean hand" would fall. We walked around the rock, then went

THE HOLY ROCK IN THE MOSQUE OF OMAR, WHERE TRADITION SAYS ABRAHAM OFFERED ISAAC UNTO THE LORD AS A SACRIFICE.

down under it, where we were shown the place made in it by Mohammed's head when he arose from prayer; also the altar of Solomon. In the centre of the holy rock is a hole which many Mohammedans believe to be inhabited by all who die in their faith, but the hole was undoubtedly made in King Solomon's time where they made their sacrifices that the blood might flow through into the brook Kedron, which runs at the foot of Mt. Mariah.—Psalms 125-2. From here we went to another Mosque, also on the grounds; here we were shown the place where "Jesus went into the Temple and taught."—St. John vii., 14. From here our guide conducted us away down under the earth to a subterranean passage, supposed to have been used as a private entrance to the Temple. In there are great blocks and pillars hewn from the solid stone, and to all appearances as perfect as the day they were placed there. Some of the stones we saw were thirty feet long, six feet deep and from eight to ten feet wide. Near here we were shown what is supposed to have been

KING SOLOMON'S STABLES,

composed of high arches of stone, covering many acres under ground; from these extended small arches. I. Kings iv., 26, "And Solomon had forty thousand stalls of horses for his chariots and twelve thousand horsemen." By the way, they are continually making new discoveries beneath the ground where once stood King Solomon's Temple. Leaving these immense grounds and excavations, and passing by the Golden Gate, we were soon by the pool of Bethesda. St. John v., 2. "Now there is at Jerusalem, by the sheep market, a pool which is called in the Hebrew tongue, Bethesda." Here we were shown two pools, but the one recently excavated is undoubtedly the real one. From the pool we went to the

JUDGMENT SEAT OF PILATE,

where Jesus was tried. "But Jesus gave him no reply!" Then Pilate said: "Speakest Thou not unto me?"—St. John xix., 9-10. Then "he brought Jesus forth, and sat down in the judgment seat, in a place that is called the pavement."—St. John x., 13. From here we went over the road where Jesus bore his cross to Calvary. St. John xix., 17, "And He bearing His Cross," to the place where He fainted on the way and "where they crucified Him." "It is finished, and He bowed His head and gave up the Ghost."—St. John xix., 30. Thus ends a noble work. "It is finished;" man is redeemed; darkness over all the earth; the veil of the Temple was rent, the earth quakes, even the rock is rent. Buried, He has arisen and ascended to Heaven, "and low I am with you always even unto the end of the world. Amen."—St. Matt. xxviii., 20. Here we leave the scenes, and with profound reverence for all that we saw in Bible land. (A few extend tour by camping out to Damascus, often getting soaking wet en route, embarking at Beyrout, while others tramp the red-hot, sunny desert as far as "Sinai;" none of this for us, as we have seen all the principal Bible sights.) At 1.30, Wednesday, December 18, we left Jerusalem for Jaffa, travelling undoubtedly over part of the road that Abraham journeyed over on his way to Egypt. Away we go over the lands of the tribe of Dan, arriving at Jaffa at 8 p. m., making the distance of forty miles in only seven and a half hours. Early Thursday morning we embark on the "Rahmaniel," an Egyptian mail steamer bound for Port Said, where we arrived early Friday morning, December 20, all well and very much pleased with our interesting tour of the

HOLY LAND.

Early Saturday morning we left Port Said for Ismailia, by an Egyptian postal steamer through the

SUEZ CANAL.

This great canal connects the Mediterranean with the Red Sea, cost nearly $100,000,000. Apart from M. de Lesseps, of Paris, the canal would never have been made; extreme length, about 100 miles; every five miles a "gare" or siding is provided so ships may pass. The Suez Canal, so far as we could see, runs through a bank of sandy desert. Looking over into Asia on our left, one sees now and then an Arab or an Egyptian and a camel. Soon we arrived at

ISMAILIA.

Is beautifully laid out. Trees have been planted on both sides of the street and have grown large, forming an arch shading the "highway;" quite pretty, you know. "All aboard;" it's now 2 p. m. and we are on an Egyptian express postal train,

and away we go for some sixty miles through a
sandy desert and the Land of Goshen, frequently
a little village of mud huts, that's about all; but
after the first sixty miles the country is fertile, for

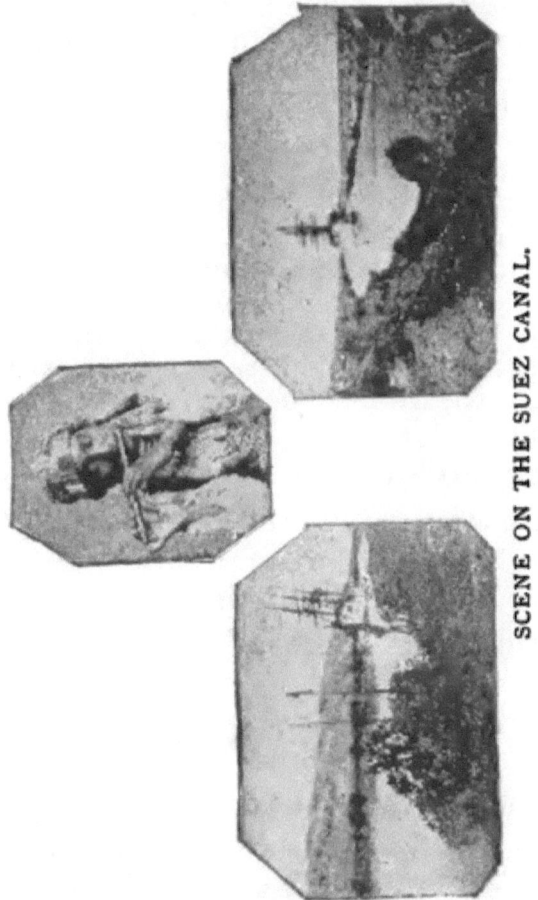

SCENE ON THE SUEZ CANAL.

it is watered from the Nile; now the country is
most beautiful, and the grass is as green as in
May in New Jersey. Everywhere the natives are
seen plowing. Yonder is a view of the pyramids,
arriving at

CAIRO, EGYPT,

at 5.30 p. m., 130 miles from Ismallia. Cairo is
perhaps the most beautiful example of a Mo-

hammedan capital. The census gives Cairo a
population of 308,108 and Egypt 6,806,381. Under
the Pharaohs Egypt was an agricultural country.
It is distinguished for the very prominent part it
played in ancient Bible history. Here Abraham
came when there was a famine in Canaan, Gen.
xii., 10. Here Joseph was brought after being
sold by his brethern, Gen. xxxvii., 23-28. Near
Cairo, along the banks of the Nile, Pharaoh's
daughter found Moses, Exodus ii., 6. Then, too
it must not be forgotten, "unto Egypt" we are
told the Virgin fled with the young child. St.
Matthew ii., 14, "He took the young child and his
mother by night and departed into Egypt."
Saturday, December 21, was a beautiful morning
and with a good two-horse carriage, driver and
dragoman, we were soon at the chief Mosque of
Cairo, the

THE MOSQUE OF SULTAN HASSAN,

which of course we entered shoeless. From here
we were driven to the

CITADEL,

and again enter another, the Mosque of Mohammed Ali, where we were shown the tomb of
Mohammed Ali, from the grounds of the Citadel
we were well paid for coming, for here we got a
splendid

BIRD'S-EYE VIEW OF CAIRO.

" He who has not seen Cairo, has not seen the
world; its soil is gold, its Nile and Pyramids a
wonder, its women are like the black-eyed virgins
of Paradise." We have now had a bird's-eye view,
all the surrounding country lies like a map before
us. Yonder, to our left, is the tomb of the "Mam-
lukes" and old Cairo, the Nile and Memphis Pyramids. - The mummies of the Pharaohs in yonder
palace. Beyond, the Great Pyramids, Sphinx and
the Sahara desert; what a glimpse of ancient his
tory! On we go to

JOSEPH'S WELL,

to where we are told Joseph came for water.
Here, no doubt, the
Pharaohs came also,
and Moses too. Deep
down 100 feet is water,
and a winding road
leads to it ; now return-
ing, and as we tread
the winding alleys
through the old ba-
zaars, a thin streak of
sky marked the narrow
space, or riding
through the streets we
see some very curious
and ancient sights.
Entering

A BIT OF CAIRO, NEAR
JOSEPH'S WELL.

SHEPHERDS' HOTEL,

we are just in time to see the Khedive pass with
his royal body-guard. He is a fine looking man
with "only one wife." Armed with a Government
permission the next day we enter the

BULAK MUSEUM.

Here we saw ancient statuary, mummies and
coffins, taken from the tombs on the banks of the
Nile. On we go to the great pyramids, and we
found the carriage road excellent all the way,
some ten miles, and shaded by large trees that
form an arch over the road. For miles we drove
along the banks of the Nile, then the river bends
and leaves us; after another little stretch we are
in front of the

GREAT PYRAMID

of Khufu (Cheops) at Giza. We looked at them with
amazement, wondering if they were built by giants.
"There were giants in the earth in those days * *
The same became mighty men." Gen. vi., 4. Did
the Bible refer to the pyramids? were they built before the flood? No one knows. It certainly required

mighty men to hew and handle such stone as we saw. From here we walked through the sand to the

SPHINX.

PYRAMIDS OF GIZA, SPHINX AND TEMPLE OF THE SPHINX.

We always sup-
posed that the
Bartholdi Statue of
Liberty in the New
York Bay, which is
137 ft. 6 in. high,
measuring f r o m
the feet to the
upper end of the
torch, to be the
largest statue in
the world. We find
we are mistaken,
for the Sphinx,
which is sculptured
out of a solid spur
of rock is larger,
for it measures 172
feet 6 inches long,
while the face or
front is fifty-six
feet high. Well, we
went around in
front and took a
good look at her
face, then descend-
ed into the temple
of the Sphinx,
which has been
recently excavated
from the sands of
t i m e ; returning,
walked all over her
back, ascended the
G r e a t Pyramid,
looked into the
King's and Queen's
chambers. But we
are dumbfounded.

OBELISK FROM ALEXANDRIA,
EGYPT.

Now at Central Park, New York
City. Gift of the late Wm.
H. Vanderbilt.

In the Great Pyramid, it is estimated, is enough
stone to build a wall four feet high, two feet thick,

from New York City to Salt Lake City, two
thousand miles. Imagine an immense four-sided
bulk of solid masonry tapering towards the sky
480 feet. The base is almost a perfect square, each
side measuring about 740 feet, and covers 13 acres.
Picture such a space; perhaps on your farm you
have a thirteen-acre field nearly square. Having
fixed your land measurements, now raise your eyes
toward heaven and imagine a solid mass of
masonry 480 feet high. We are told it took 300,-
000 men between twenty and thirty years to build.
Inside the Great Pyramid are two large chambers,
called the King's and Queen's Chambers. Entering,
the masonry is as perfect as when placed there,
nobody knows when. Immense stones were used,
some thirty feet long, ten feet wide, eight or ten
feet deep. It is said the stone was brought here
from a quarry some twenty miles. Now leaving
one of the wonders of the world we drive to the

KHEDIVE'S PALACE,

or the new Giza museum. Here we looked upon
the faces of the mummies of the Pharaohs. They
are guarded carefully; while one man leads the

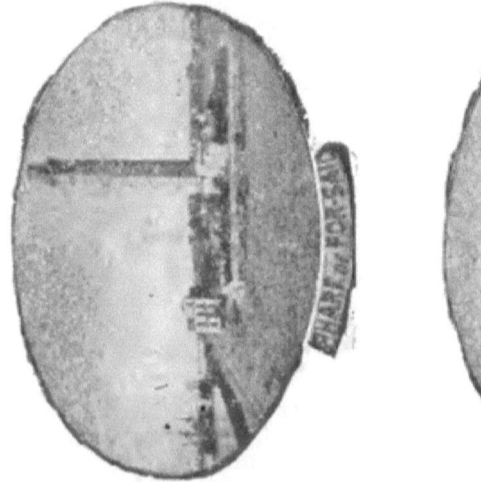

way, two follow closely on your heels. The new
museum will be the finest in the world when com-

pleted. It was with some difficulty that we got into it at all; there was a good deal of "red tape." At 9 a. m., promptly, December 25th, we turned our backs upon Cairo, with her gay amusements, the Pyramids, Sphinx—the wonders of the world. Turning our faces from the ghastly sight of the mummies of the Pharaohs, and as the express train speeds along, we take a side look at the great Pyramids. The morning sun had thrown its rays upon them and they seem to say:

"Time mocks all things, but we laugh at time."

Onward flies our Egyptian express, till, 1.30 p.m., we arrive at Ismailia, where we embarked on the

P. & O. STEAMER "KHEDIVE"

the following morning at 5.21. Rather early, but we were well repaid when we saw her coming, the great electric search light reaching far out into the canal; it was a pretty sight. Entering the " Bitter Lakes," we arrive at the Suez at 2 p. m. The bay was as pretty as a picture. But we did not tarry at Suez (population 10,913); soon we are steaming down the gulf. The good ship is beautifully trimmed with flags, etc., for yesterday was Christmas. " Here is Moses well to the left." The hills now on both sides look barren, no signs of vegetation; in the distance, a long way off, is

MOUNT SINAI,
where Moses received the Ten Commandments; a hill on the African side has streaks of very red clay, and looks volcanic, but there are no volcanos here. Beyond is the river Nile, which flows over 1,000 miles without a single tributary. Somewhere here the children of Israel crossed the Red Sea; nobody seems to

CONVENT AND MOUNT SINAI.

know exactly where—Exodus xiv., 21-28. Now the rocks "Two Brothers" are sighted. Friday, Saturday and Sunday, the thermometer registered 85 to 87 in the shade at 9 a. m. The Captain, who locks like **ex-President** Hayes, **exclaimed** it was hot enough to roast eggs in the sun. No wonder, for on either side of the Red Sea **are great** deserts. **Here** we are even with

MECCA,

where Mohammed Ali was born. All good Mohammedans, you know, pray with their faces toward Mecca, and whose evening call to prayer is "Allahu Akbar." There is no God but God. Mohammed is the Apostle of God. "Come to prayer, come to salvation; Allahu Akbar, Lailaha illa-illah." Sixty thousand gallons of wine is drunk annually at communion tables in America ("Water into wine," John ii., 1-11). There are 1,000 different confessions of faith in the world, and 3,064 languages spoken. The entire population of the globe is twelve hundred million, of whom 35,214,000 die every year, 96,480 every day, 4,020 every hour, 67 every minute. On the other hand, the births amount to 36,792,000 every year, 100,800 every day, 4,200 every hour, and 70 every minute. You may ask, Where do they all go? Our answer must be, Is there any end to space? Remember, too, of this vast army of human beings there are no two exactly alike. There is a supposition that

HEAVEN,

is one of the Pleiades (one of a group of seven stars, commonly called "Seven Sisters" from its remarkable attraction, recently discovered by astronomers). This star is mentioned in the Holy Bible, as follows: "Then the Lord answered Job * * * (Job xxxviii., 1): Canst Thou bind the sweet influence of Pleiades" (Job xxxviii., 31). Who but the Lord knew of the "sweet influence?" Certainly man did not. These stars are visible at certain times in both hemispheres—of course, remember this is only supposition. Well, we have passed the "Twelve Apostles," twelve rocks in the Red Sea. To our left is Arabia, where

VIEW IN THE RED SEA.
(Our good ship passing the Twelve Apostles at midnight.)

15,000,000 manage to live; heat intense. To our right Africa; nobody knows her population. At 10 p. m. Perim is sighted, well fortified by the British. Entering the Bay of

ADEN, IN INDIA,

early Tuesday morning, December 31, 1889. Here lies anchored the celebrated English man-of-war, "Calliope," which recently steamed out of the great cyclone off Samoa, an island in the Pacific, while the American and German men-of-war were all lost. Entering Aden from the sea reminds one of Gibraltar. Aden although in Arabia really belongs and is called "Aden, India," being governed by India. The natives are nearly naked, as the heat here is intense; no rain has fallen here during the last three years, and they have been known to have been without rain for seven years. We were not favorably impressed with rocky old Aden; and soon we are steaming out into the Gulf of Aden, into the

ARABIAN SEA,

passing Cape Guardafui, the last bit of Africa, on our right and Socotra, an island in the sea, on our left. From November to March the Arabian Sea is always "moderate and fine;" we find it nearly as smooth as glass all the way to

COLOMBO, CEYLON,

where we arrive Tuesday, January 7, 1890, at 8 p.m., being by sea 7,058 miles from London, or 10,519 miles from New York City via Glasgow. The view approaching Colombo from the sea is fine. Population, 111,942. The island of Ceylon is about twice the size of New Jersey. Steaming behind the great breakwaters, we find the heat unbearable, the humidity the greatest we ever experienced either in Europe or America. As we landed on the pier there was the Hon. Joseph Pulitzer, proprietor of the New York *World*, who looked "red hot" in his big helmet. About the weather, in an interview with a reporter of the *Times* of Ceylon, January 7, the great newspaper man replied: "Oh, well, you can see me all right here; I am half naked, and all together uncomfortable in this heat." Approaching us he said: "Well, Mayor Beatty, what are you doing away over here? ain't you lost?" "Doing? why, I am making a tour of the world." "Oh, I see." After exchanging the compliments of the season, and informing him that we were at the laying of the corner stone of Pulitzer's *World* Building before our departure, he continued: "Do you know the building has already reached its eleventh story?" The *World* man and ex-Congressman said he would sail for Calcutta at once, by the "Khedive," which was the steamer that brought us from Egypt. Bidding each other "bon voyage" we separate, and away went the *World* man for his steamer, with his doctor, secretary and two native servants. Taking a carriage we pass the Governor's residence, barracks and beautiful rocks along the beach. Now we are on the "Galle Face" road by the sea; it is very pretty, reminding one of "on the beach at Long Branch" only ten times nicer. Pass the museum to the "Cinnamon Gardens," perhaps the finest tropical garden of the kind in the world. Now we are driving down the Fifth Avenue of Colombo, where we saw some of the most beautiful lawns and tropical scenery in front of residences that mortal man ever beheld; Egypt was nowhere. "There you are," exclaimed our 240-pound guide, who looked the picture of the late Wm. H. Vanderbilt, as he pointed to Slave Island Lake. It was beautiful. Now crossing the railway to Kandy and Nuwara Elija, where it is said the coolies work for sixteen cents per day, supporting a large family, subsisting on

CURRY AND RICE.

The men natives let their hair grow long, and do it up in a knot at the back of the head the same as the women, placing in the hair on top of the head a curved tortoise shell comb. Frequently we see them wearing no hat at all. One can scarcely tell the males from the females. We intended to have remained in Ceylon two weeks, then taking a side trip to Calcutta, Benares, Delhi, etc., embarking at Bombay for Australia, but the heat was so intense at Colombo that we feared to make the journey. After seeing all of Colombo worth seeing we embarked on the

P. AND O. STEAMER "PARAMATTA,"

crossing the equator at 5 a. m., Friday, January 10, on our way to a cooler climate, as Ceylon, we must certainly agree with the "*World* man," is "altogether uncomfortable." By the way, we did not see the line while

CROSSING THE EQUATOR,

nor were our feet chalked, nor were we tarred
and feathered, as is said was the custom in former
days; on the contrary, an orchestra played six airs

LEAVING CEYLON BOUND FOR AUSTRALIA.
(Adams Peak in the distance.)

during the forenoon. Thursday, Friday, Saturday and Sunday, January 9, 10, 11 and 12—The
sky is cloudy, and at times it rained very hard,
for we have entered the northwest or middle mon-
soon. On we go through the

INDIAN OCEAN,

whose mighty body of water covers 25,000,000
square miles, while the land area of North and
South America is only 15,745,576. On our return
to America we shall cross the Pacific, 67,800,000
square miles. What hidden treasures lie deep
buried under these vast bodies of water! How
many steamers and sailing vessels there are who
have left a safe harbor with many human beings,

valuable cargo, etc., who never afterward have
been heard from—gone down, perhaps, in a storm,
a collision, fire or cyclone, maybe, as it were, in a
twinkling of an eye. The greatest depth of the
ocean of which soundings have been taken is off
the coast of Japan. At that point the water is
five miles deep, and at the bottom traces of ani-
mal life have been found.

Before leaving America, we applied for a

PASSPORT,

part of which reads: "Safely and freely to pass,
and in case of need to give him all lawful aid and
protection." Well, so far we have had no occa-
sion to use it. We passed everywhere "safely
and freely," nor have we needed "lawful aid and
protection." However, thanks to Uncle Sam for
this safeguard. Every evening now the

SOUTHERN CROSS

is visible. It is composed of four very brilliant
fixed stars, forming a perfect cross, with two
bright "Centaur" stars, who never weary pointing at the cross, which is the mariner's guide in
the southern latitude, the same as the "north
star" is in the northern. All the way from Colombo to nearly King George's Sound, Australia, a
distance of nearly 4,000 miles, not a sign of a ship
do we see; now and then a shark and a few flying
fish, that's all. Now Cape Leeuwin is sighted,
a dangerous coast, where, we are sorry to say,
there is no lighthouse. Approaching

WESTERN AUSTRALIA,

soon after leaving the cape, the shore looks
scrubby, with here and there patches of sand.
Some twenty miles further on reminds us of
the coast of Ireland, as we steam toward Queens-
town from America—especially the rocks; of
course, it is not so green. A run of thirty miles
further one sees great bluffs, similar to the Palis-
ades on the Hudson River, New York; some ten

miles more, and it is the picture of the Highlands below Sandy Hook, New Jersey. Steaming up King George's Sound, fringed with snow-white sand, the sight was very fine. Arriving at

ALBANY

January 19, 1890, at 5 P. M., being from England 10,950 miles, or 14,411 miles from New York City via Glasgow. Strolling through the streets we find them wide and dusty. The town is situated on rising ground, at the foot of Mount Clarence and Melville, population 2,000, and is 261 miles southeast of Perth, population 5,044, the capital of

ALBANY, KING GEORGE'S SOUND, SOUTH AUSTRALIA.

Western Australia. The men wear great widebrim slouch hats. In the interior of Western Australia are the Great Sandy and Victoria Deserts, and many dry salt lakes. At certain times of the year these lakes are filled with water; at other seasons they are simply a dry cake of salt, white as snow and used for eating purposes. Poison grass abounds in many places fatal to cattle and sheep.

Western Australia is the largest division of Australia, being 1,490 miles long, 850 wide. The last census gives the number of inhabitants of this vast tract of land at 29,708. Fertile land exists here only in patches, the greater portion of the country being sand, scrub and great forests. Leaving Albany January 20, we proceed across the great Australia Bight. New York City lies directly under the Bight. If the reader doubts this let him examine a globe (not a map) of the world. Of course we must be then half way around the world, via Australia. December, January and February is summer in Australia; springtime in North America means autumn here, and autumn, spring, just the opposite of North America, Europe, Asia, etc. The further south we go the colder it gets. Over the Bight merrily we go (for here we are royally entertained by orchestra, tableaux and play, best we ever witnessed at sea), through Investigator's Straits, pass Spencer's Gulf and Cape, side Kangaroo Island, up Gulf St. Vincent past Glenelg, along side of

SOUTH AUSTRALIA,

where 293,509 people live, whose area of square miles is 903,690, or nearly four times larger than Texas, where copper and iron ores are mined, and great forests of gum trees, fertile lands, grape vineyards, etc., abound. But alas, in the interior often five years drouth are known, dry salt lakes, Ross and other deserts are found. On we go to a pier near Semaphore, thence ten miles by rail via Port Adelaide, arriving at

ADELAIDE,

the capital, population 38,479, January 23, 1890, at 12 noon. Adelaide lies on a level plain at the foot of several hills; streets wide, clean, and many nicely shaded; houses built of stone, marble and

brick; double deck two horse street cars.
Passing House of Parliament, Royal Exchange,
Town Hall, Post Office by carriage up King
William Street to Royal Courts, thence through
the suburbs to the Royal Botanic Gardens and
Zoo, over forty acres; returning via the Cattle and
Jubilee Exhibition Buildings, entering the Arcade

and stores. We found the citizens extremely
polite and obliging. Average heat of Adelaide,
January, 1890 (summer), 106 shade, 147 sun, hottest
season ever known. Rather too hot for us, and at
6 p. m. we steam away. Near Cape Jervis, over
Encounter Bay we go, passing to our left Nelson,
Portland, etc., up Phillips Bay, surrounded by the
lands of **VICTORIA, AUSTRALIA,**
whose area of square miles is 87,884, or nearly as
large as England, Scotland, Wales and Ireland

combined. Here we are lashed fast to Williams-
town Pier, Saturday, Jan. 25, 12.05 noon, ten
miles south of Melbourne, near where you may
drop a lead seven fathoms at low tide. There to
our right lies the great Australian city. Nothing
to suggest it, however, excepting Exhibition Building dome, steeples and far away haze of her
smoke. Now taking a special Royal train, we
wind the bay horseshoe fashion, passing many
one-story frame houses at Beach, Newport, Foots-
cray (here we see to our left an Australian race
course), etc., stepping out upon an ordinary platform, at

MELBOURNE.

We have nothing to remind us that we are in so
large and so handsomely built a city, as the houses
at the station are low and ordinary, excepting

THE GRAND HOTEL, MELBOURNE, VICTORIA, AUSTRALIA.

hacks, carriages, etc. Melbourne, the capital of
Victoria, population 291,464, and with her suburbs
nearly half a million, is certainly a very enterprising and American style city, for her people dress,

act and speak like Americans, her streets are broad, and the cable American style tramway system is perfect; traveling the streets of Melbourne one could easily imagine they were in

BOTANICAL GARDENS, MELBOURNE, VICTORIA, AUSTRALIA.

Chicago, Ill. Melbourne was founded in 1836. The rapidity of its growth is historical; all that enterprise, talent and gold can produce has been carried out here to its utmost. Imagine a city of one hundred miles of streets, straight and wide, many planted with trees; an area of seven square miles, beautiful parks and botanical gardens, great and handsome buildings built on little hills looking like a level plain from the bay, and you have Melbourne. Well, at 1.37 p. m., Wednesday, January 29, we left Melbourne for Sydney, New South Wales. Out of Phillips Bay we go through Bass Straits; to our right is Tasmania and to our left Victoria; now rounding Cape Howe into the South Pacific Ocean we go, and soon we are sailing up Port Jackson, one of the most beautiful and safe harbors to be found in the world. No pen can describe the many beautiful changes of scenery as our good ship glides to her pier, arriving at

SYDNEY, N. S. W.,

Friday, January 31, at 4 p. m. Sydney is the capital seat of government of New South Wales;

A BIT OF THE BOTANICAL GARDENS, SYDNEY, N. S. W., AUSTRALIA.

it is the site of the first settlement in Australia, and is built on the southern shores of Port Jackson. Port Jackson is only eight miles long, but its coast line measures 165 miles, being indented here and there with pretty bays. Here in Sydney we find beautiful gardens and parks, miles of winding streets, massive and well-built buildings and warehouses that would be a credit to any city; population about 300,000.

After arranging for our passage to New Zealand, Honolulu and San Francisco, on February 1, a stroll was made through the principal streets of Sydney, and during a week's stay here excursions were made to Bondi and Coogee, beautiful side suburbs. The views here were grand; huge perpendicular rocks rise high above the great Pacific, and breakers that often rise fifty feet. Now down Sydney harbor we go to Manly Beach, a fine sea coast, and as our steamer speeds along a magnificent view is obtained of the Governor's residence, Botanical Gardens, Watson Bay, and a peep into Middle Harbor. Our week's stay at Sydney is now ended, and on February 7 away we go along the Parramatta River, through the town bearing its name, on an Australian express train to Penrith, near where we cross the Nepean River, on whose smooth waters Beach defeated Hanlon for the championship of the world. Shortly after leaving Penrith the ascent of the

BLUE MOUNTAINS OF AUSTRALIA

is commenced by the "little zig-zag," and as the train passes from zig to zag an extended view is obtained of the Emu Plains, Nepean River and agricultural valley below, dotted here and there with orange groves. Thirty-six miles away lies Sydney. Now the train enters a deep cut and winds the mountains right and left, then along the edge of a deep precipice, where one can look down nearly 3,000 feet below into the Kanimbla Valley. Now a glimpse of the valley of the Grouse, with her huge cliffs extending 3,000 feet toward the heavens, as we see them from the valley below, until 1.55 p. m.

MOUNT VICTORIA

is reached, being 3,422 feet above the level of the Pacific Ocean.   Here we tarry for five days to see

THE GREAT ZIG-ZAG OVER THE BLUE MOUNTAINS,
NEW SOUTH WALES, AUSTRALIA.

the wonderful sights in these mountains. The first place we visit is the "great zig-zag," ninety-two miles west of Sydney, on the northern dividing range—this wonderful piece of engineering cost $125,000 per mile—thence to Mount Piddington we go, to get an extensive view of the valley below, then down the little zig-zag to

BUSHRANGER'S CAVES.

Entering, one fancies he sees one of the old bushrangers making for him, so dark and dismal are the surroundings. The engineer's cascade is next visited, which is quite pretty, also the road to Mt. York, etc., but the greatest sight of all is

GOVETT'S LEAP,

near Blackheath. Approaching to a point of rock in front is an awful gulf, 3,000 feet below; an immense valley we see, walled in by perpendicular cliffs, stretching away as far as the eye can reach into the valley of the Grouse. At the bottom is a perfect sea of foliage, huge trees that look like small shrubs. To the right is the leap or falls, which descend 520 feet without a break. As the mist arose from the falls below, before us is a beautiful rainbow. What a magnificent sight!

At Katoomba Falls we descend deep down under them, in order to see them properly. Near by is the "Orphan Rock," 1,000 feet high; over beyond are the "Three Sisters." In the valley below, 3,000 feet, is seen the Katoomba coal mines, with its clustering village where the miners live, some of whom, it is said, have never been out of this deep chasm. On approaching the

WENTWORTH FALLS,

some four miles from Katoomba, a winding foot-path leads the way down the mountain side to a point of rock extending some ten feet beyond the falls. Down deep, over a vast amphitheatre of rock, we see this fearful leap of water, first over a cataract, headlong it goes over three great

GOVETT'S LEAP, BLUE MOUNTAINS.

GOVETT'S LEAP, 3000 FEET. BLUE MOUNTAINS, NEW SOUTH WALES, AUSTRALIA.

falls, some 1,200 feet, to the valley below. The clouds had lifted over the scene just as we approached. It was a magnificent sight. To our right now we wind our way among the cliffs of the rocks to the never weary "Weeping Rock." Returning to Sydney, February 14, we take the beautiful

"ILLAWARRA LINE,"

passing near by Botany Bay, where Captain Cook, it is said, first landed in 1770, over George River, skirting the National Park, Clifton, Bulli Pass, near Fitzroy Falls and Kangaroo Valley, Wollongong to Kiama, seventy miles south of Sydney, the present terminus of this wild and romantic line, to the

"BLOWHOLE"

we go, to see a crater where water spouts often a hundred feet high from a subterranean passage below, roaring like distant thunder, a curious sight. Returning again to Sydney, over the North Line we go, crossing the Parramatta River to the famous

HAWKESBURY RIVER,

being thirty-six miles north of Sydney, a very picturesque river, reminding one of the beautiful lakes of Killarney, Ireland, forming, as it does in its course, many pretty bays, almost surrounded by green hills ; to reach this part you pass through six tunnels in less than six miles. Time flies, and we must not weary our readers. Well, New South Wales has an area of 316,320 square miles, or nearly four times as large as Victoria, Australia. The interior of N. S. W. is a great sheep growing country; a fellow-passenger, who occupies 750,000 acres, owns 1,500,000 sheep and 10,000 cattle, informed me that he had no debts— of course he must be a millionaire. Australia, as everybody knows, grows the finest wool in the world. February 19, at 4 p. m., while the good

people of New Jersey are asleep, for it's one
o'clock in the morning in New Jersey, we steam

BRIDGE OVER THE BEAUTIFUL "HAWKESBURY RIVER,"
NEAR SYDNEY, N. S. WALES, AUSTRALIA.

out into the South Pacific Ocean, through the

SYDNEY HARBOR, FROM NORTH HEAD.
Our good ship leaving Sydney Harbor, N. S. W.
"Out into the great Pacific Ocean we go."

South and North Heads, on the Oceanic Steam-
ship Co.'s steamer

"ALAMEDA,"

bidding good-bye to Australia, after having
visited all the colonies, excepting Queensland,
which is entirely too hot to visit at this season of
the year. This steamer, the "Alameda," that takes
us away from the shores of Australia, brought
Lord Carrington, Governor of N. S. W., from
New Zealand a fortnight ago. One thing, this
steamer, owned by an American company, is well
built, roomy and clean, and a better table we
have yet to find at sea. Now approaching North
End,

NEW ZEALAND,

we are reminded of the coast near Holyhead,
Wales. Further around towards Auckland is seen

immense bluffs; to our left is Great Barrier Island, and single, dangerous rocks peep up out of the Pacific. Entering the Hauraki Gulf, to our right is seen the celebrated hot springs of Waiwera, and the broad waters of the Firth of Thames to our left. Now we are sailing up the harbor, dotted here and there by beautiful residences and pine trees. Yonder is Mount Eden, an extinct Volcano; the approach to the city is very pretty. Well, February 23 we arrive at

AUCKLAND,

a city of some 40,000 inhabitants, streets broad, well and substantially built buildings, two-horse street cars, with one of the best steamboat piers in the world. Strolling up Queen St. we wind our way, visiting the many sights of the city, thence to "Jacob's Ladder," at the base of "Old Bloody Sky" or Mount Eden, an extnict volcano, the principle sight. Winding our way zig-zag fashion, near the top we pause to look into the crater, which reminds us of Mt. Vesuvius, Italy. Now climbing still higher, to the very pinnacle, we get a grand bird's-eye view of Auckland and surrounding country; here one can see away across New Zealand from ocean to ocean. Here lies at our feet Auckland and her magnificent harbor; yonder is Mount Albert, another extinct Volcano. Auckland is built upon a volcanic isthmus; within a radius of ten miles of the city Hockstetter discovered 63 points of eruption; of course at the present time they are extinct, the principal one being old "Bloody Sky."

THE MAORIS.

The tradition of the natives, the Maoris, is shrouded in mystery; nobody in Auckland or anywhere else seems to know their origin. When Captain Cook landed in 1770 there were some 90,000 in New Zealand, now it is said only 40,000 survive; thus the Maoris, like the volcanos, are fast becoming extinct; originally they were man-eaters, and fed on rats, dogs, etc., but now they are becoming civilized and are to be seen walking the streets of Auckland. Approaching one I asked him if he could speak English. He tipped his hat and smiled, but made no reply, poor fellow; his countenance seemed to speak louder than words, "Our race is fast passing away." Leaving "Old Bloody Sky," we took another look into her great crater, which once was a mass of liquid fire; it is now cold and silent, and cattle were grazing on its steep sides, and two little girls had wandered their way along the crater. When asked why they were here, replied: "Oh, mister, we are on our way to a picnic, just on the other side of the mountain." New Zealand covers an area of 105,342 square miles, or about thirteen times larger than New Jersey. Her mountain scenery ranks among the grandest in the world. Here we find snow-capped peaks—Mt. Cook, the Mt. Blanc of the New Zealand Alps, being 13,200 feet high—immense glaziers eighteen miles long by two broad, bluffs, etc. The pink and white terraces, recently destroyed by an earthquake, were said to have been one of the wonders of the world. Here we find fertile lands, where wheat, oats and flax in large quantities are yielded annually, supplying her sister colonies with wheat and oats. It is also a great sheep-growing country; the climate is pleasant, rainfall far better than in Australia. Wellington, the capital and seat of government, lies in the south. This year Duneden has an exhibition, but as we have visited the Paris Exhibition of 1878 and 1889 we think it not worth our while to visit this. We steam out into the Southern Pacific Ocean on our way to

TUTUILA., SAMOA.

Tuesday, February 25, we are near the 180th meridian, and this of course is Tuesday. The next day, about 9 a. m., we cross the meridian,

Before nine o clock it was Wednesday morning, but immediately after crossing it we are set back a day and find it is again Tuesday, February 25, making really one day and night forty-eight hours; thus traveling around the world east we gain a day, while going west a day is lost. As we steam along to the left of us is the

KERMADIC,

a group of seven islands, and we are told they are not inhabited. If this is so, here is a chance for emigration. The largest is said to be twelve miles in circumference. It is a belief that in former ages Australia extended far beyond its present limits, and that a great continent once existed, perhaps as large as Africa and Asia combined, where only a remnant composed of seven island groups are now to be found. After all, the Australasian colonies, seven in number, covering an area of 3,075,135 square miles, had only 3,091,897 human beings residing here in 1883, and have only increased about 1,000,000 since. A vast country, nearly as large as the United States, which has an area of 3,547,000 square miles, while the present estimated population of the United States is 64,000,000, and the annual growth by natural causes and immigration is placed at 1,000,000. On we go steaming on the coast of

POLYNESIA,

passing through the Friendly, Hapai, group of islands. We found them very friendly, for the water and weather, as we steamed through them, was all that one could desire; the balmy breezes were delightful. Here, to our left, we go near the group of the 250

FIJI ISLANDS, POLYNESIA,

discovered by Tasman, a Dutch navigator in 1646, area 8,000 square miles, or nearly as large as Massachusetts. All the Fiji group rise steeply from the sea; they are hilly rather than mountainous, although the highest peak rises 4,000 feet; hurricanes are numerous; heat, summer 120 shade, and sixty the lowest in winter; population, native 115,000; Europeans 3,500, and immigrants 9,600. The natives are probably the finest species of the dark race of the Pacific, being tall and robust, hair and beard frizzled. Fruits, including pineapples, bananas, cocoanuts, limes, lemons, tomatoes, bread fruits, etc., are raised in great quantities, exporting $2,000,000 worth annually. Living in a country where nearly all their wants are supplied by nature, wearing little or no clothing, the Fiji has little need to labor; rainfall is abundant, climate healthy, but evidences of volcanic eruptions are everywhere visible. Fiji is under British rule, raising $500,000 annually for the Crown, which is obtained from customs license, etc. Sura is the seat of government; on the whole we have seen worse places than these islands.

TUTUILA, SAMOA.

The approach to these beautiful islands of the sea, Friday, February 28, was exceedingly fine, especially when we saw the little canoes filled with natives making an exciting race for our steamer; and before one is aware of it they are on deck, offering us many curiosities for sale. They are copper-colored people, exceedingly well built, very polite, and it is said honest and honorable in all their dealings. Like the Fijis, nature supplies them with an abundance of food, and wearing very little clothing, they too need not work very hard for a living. The island is everywhere green with vegetation; cocoanut and banana trees are to be seen on every side, and the shores are dotted here and there with native straw huts. Yonder lies anchored the "Adams," an American man-of-war; beyond is the scene of the dreadful cyclone which occurred here about a year ago, so familiar in the world's history, which really did settle the dispute between powerful nations, putting the native

TEMDINOKA AT HOME—AN EVENING SCENE IN HIS PALACE.

king back upon his throne. Well, early Monday morning, March 3, we crossed the

EQUATOR,

and found the air balmy and the sea all that one could desire.

A WATER SPOUT.

Looking westward, Thursday, March 5, we saw a tremendous water spout, reaching to the very clouds, that hung darkly, mountain-peak style, upside down. Of this awful and curious sight an officer, who has travelled the ocean for the past thirteen years, said it was the largest he ever saw, and that it must have weighed hundreds of tons, being a mile in diameter; he continued that if it had struck our ship it would have gone through the upper deck as easily as he could have put his finger through a newspaper. The phenomena was followed by a great fall of rain, and very heavy sea, blowing at times almost a hurricane. The following morning, through the thick mist, an outline of a mountain peak on the Hawaiian Islands was faintly visible. Arriving off Honolulu, we

MONUMENT IN FRONT OF GOVERNMENT BUILDING, HONOLULU HAWAIIAN ISLANDS.

could not enter the harbor, for the mountain-like waves that played around her coast. For

A COCOANUT GROVE, HAWAIIAN ISLANDS.

twenty-four hours we laid outside in a heavy sea, tossing about like a feather, reminding us of our experience at Jaffa. An officer who has landed here ninety-four times said he never knew this to happen before, and that this was the first time in seven years that the "Alameda" could not go to her dock at once. At last the pilot ventured out through the great waves and breakers, and we are safely conducted through the dangerous coral reefs at

HONOLULU, OAHU.

Upon landing we learned that the city and surrounding country had had the greatest rain storm known here for fifteen years. The railway was washed out in many places, no trains were running; the road to "Pali" and "Punchbowl" was impassible, two of the principal sights here. Of course we had to view them from a distance. However, we were able to drive to

WAIKIKI,

a seaside resort at the base of the old Diamond Point, an extinct volcano, passing on our way the King's palace, government buildings, pretty residences, rice fields, banana and cocoanut groves, tropical gardens, reminding one of Ceylon, only the natives here all wear clothing. Here a stroll was made along the beautiful coast and King's Park, etc. The climate of Honolulu is delightful, never too hot or too cold the whole year around, and the soil is exceedingly fertile and productive in the valleys, and almost every house in the city has a telephone. Of course Honolulu lies at the foot of several large mountains, which are of volcanic formation, population 7,000, and the group of fifteen islands have a population of 57,985, and the whole contains 6,667 square miles. Here is the

HOUSE OF FIRE,

being the greatest active volcano in the world. Leaving the city the mountains look barren and volcanic. Here is one that is shaped just like the Great Pyramid of Egypt. To our right as we steam along is

MOLOKAI,

where there is a leprous settlement in a valley entirely surrounded by mountains, and the only way to reach it is by sea. On we go, leaving behind this dreadful sight of human misery, through the North Pacific Ocean. Approaching the great continent of

NORTH AMERICA,

and especially the United States, we felt like exclaiming—

"My country, 'tis of thee,
Sweet land of liberty,"

for no land looked so dear to us. Now, approaching the Golden Gate, passing to our right the Cliff House, and the rocks covered with many seals on the shore of the Northern Pacific, and along the cliffs we see a passenger train shooting through the tunnel, etc., up the great San Francisco Bay we go, and at 5 p. m., Saturday, March 15, we are safely landed once more on American soil, and in less than an hour are comfortably settled at the

PALACE HOTEL,

said to be the largest and most magnificent hotel in the world. The city presents a broken appearance, owing to the hills; population about 300,000. Soon we are on our way to the Golden Gate Park and Cliff House, where we saw hundreds of sea lions, barking and sunning themselves on the rocks; returning, we visited the millionaire "bonanza-kings'" residences and Chinatown; one thing sure, San Francisco street car cable system is perfect, for they climb the steep hills like magic. Crossing the bay, Tuesday, March 18, on one of the largest ferryboats in the world, to Oakland, just opposite; population 34,555. Soon we are on a Central Pacific express train, flying along the shore of the San Francisco Bay, passing to our right fine fertile land, until Port Costa

CLIFF HOUSE.

GOLDEN GATE

is reached, where we cross **over to** Benicia on the Solano, the largest railroad steam ferryboat in

the world, capable of carrying eighty-four cars
and two locomotives at one time. On we go,
passing through the richest fertile land in California, arriving at

A CALIFORNIA GARDEN IN MIDWINTER.

SACRAMENTO,

the capital; population last census 21,420. Here
a visit was paid to the Capitol buildings, a magnificent structure, reminding us of our national
Capitol. The residences, and especially the cathe-

HOTEL NEAR THE SEA OF ICE.

dral, were **very pretty**. California, or the
"Golden State," area 158,360 square miles, is the
second largest State in the Union. It is said to be

one of the richest agricultural tracts in the United States, very rich soil and favorable climate, for often two crops have been yielded in a single year. It is also very picturesque, the Yosemite Valley (like Wentforth falls aud cliffs, Australia) and large trees being among the finest scenery in the world.

Well, space forbids our telling all we saw in California, and we hasten on, leaving Sacramento Wednesday, March 10, by a vestibule Pullman car, and soon are climbing the great Sierra Nevada Mountains till the very summit is reached, 7,017 feet; here we begin to descend, through numerous tunnels and some seventy-five miles of snow sheds. Now we are rounding Cape Horn, one of the grandest scenes in the world, one look in the awful chasm (like Govett's Leap) being sufficient to unsettle anyone's nerves. But time flies and on we go to Truckee, where we stop for breakfast; back of us are seen the great mountains, where the snow is 80 feet deep; here, twelve miles south of Lake Tahoe, which is exceedingly beautiful. On we go, now and then is seen the "poor Indian," who like the Maoris are fast becoming extinct. "Old Gabriel, an Indian chief, has just gone to his long home, at the age of 151 years," so says the San Francisco Chronicle of March 17, 1890; nobody believed he would ever die, for he had outlived all his children, grandchildren and generation. At Reno, Nevada, we took the trouble to get off the express train and try to talk with a band of Indians that were huddled near the platform, gazing at the "iron horse." We asked one if he could speak English; he put his finger in his mouth, not a smile on his face, as much as to say: "You palefaces have robbed us of our land and homes." Here, at Reno, one must change for Carson City and Virginia City, the great gold and silver region. The "sage hen" State of Nevada, area 110,700 square miles, is rich in minerals, for Comstock lode is supposed to be the richest silver mine

CHIEFS OF THE SOUTHERN UTES.   (SEE PAGE 85.)

in the world; but her mountains as we pass along
look barren and volcanic, and for miles we travel
over the great Nevada desert, which we are informed is rich soil when irrigated.   At

HUMBOLDT

the porter calls out "twenty minutes for dinner."
Near here is the Humboldt range, on which the
snow continues to hold its icy sway the whole
year round.   This is a thrifty town, as the soil
has been irrigated from the Humboldt River,
which, by the way, we have been following for
some miles.   Near by are the Mud, Pyramid,
Humboldt, Winnemucca and Carson Lakes; to
our right, as we leave the station, is seen hot sul-

phur springs. Near here is a mine of pu.
sulphur. The train speeds on through about the
same scenery until we find ourselves skirting the

GREAT SALT LAKE, UTAH,

the mysterious Dead Sea of America, 126 miles
long, 45 wide, which we follow for 5 miles until

OGDEN, UTAH,

is reached, and we find that we have traveled 833
miles, being the distance from San Francisco.
Ogden is a very enterprising and pretty city, but
we must not tarry. Crossing the Weber River,
alongside of Salt Lake, to Hot Springs, some 38
miles, the great Mormon city is reached, and the
porter calls out

SALT LAKE CITY,

where we arrived Thursday, March 20. On leaving the train we learn that this city is enjoying a
" boom," and no wonder, for its streets are broad
and its electric tramway system is all that could
be desired; population over 30,000. Everything
indicated prosperity. Strolling up a street we
pause to view the residences of the late Brigham
Young and his wives; a little further on his tomb.
marked by a plain slab and enclosed by an iron
fence; outside of this iron railing lie several of
his wives, the whole enclosed by a low stone fence.
Returning past the great Mormon printing office
we enter the grounds of the new temple, which
cost some $10,000,000. Into the immense Mormon
Tabernacle we go, the largest building of the kind
in the world, having a seating capacity of 10,000,
yet from one end to the other you can hear a pin
drop. There are no pillars in the centre of the
building, its vast dome-like roof having no visible
support. Its organ is said to be one of the largest
in the world. Utah has an area of 84,900 square
miles, or nearly as large as England, Scotland, Ireland and Wales combined, and is fertile when irrigated, as rainfall is uncertain. The Mormons de-

serve great credit in this respect, as they have turned a desert into a blooming garden. Leaving

MORMON TEMPLE, TABERNACLE AND ASSEMBLY HALL, SALT LAKE CITY, UTAH.

here Friday, March 21, we turn our backs upon the great Mormon city. Winding alongside of the Jor-

dan River up the Jordan narrow we go, leaving to
our right huge mountains, near the "Dead Sea."
Passing Mt. Aspinwall, 11,011 feet high, near
American Fork, on to Provo, Springville, on our
express train goes, and we soon find ourselves
thundering up the

SPANISH FORK CANON,

one of the grandest gorges of the Wasatch
Mountains. The formation of the rocks here are

A HOME OF A CLIFF DWELLER.

volcanic and are certainly very interesting; the Spanish Fork River flows madly through toward the Utah Lake below. Soon we reach Soldier Summit, elevation 7,465 feet; on we go, passing Pleasant Valley Junction, into the deep gorge of the Price River, entering the "Gates Ajar" or the

"CASTLE GATE,"

huge cliffs that look like the gates to an old castle, which are the outposts of the Wasatch Mountains; a little further on one sees rocks resembling the ruins of castles, now other rocks look like the walls around Jerusalem; it was a grand and curious sight. Here we are at Price, Fort Dushane; an Indian reservation is eighty miles north of here, and is 135 miles south from Fort Bridger, and comprises 4,000,000 acres and occupied by about 2,500 Indians. Arriving at Green River Station, where we break our journey, resting for the night at a good hotel in the Utah deserts; everything here belongs to the railroad company. Early Saturday morning, March 22, we leave here, crossing the Green River, through the Utah desert, nearly all the land being rich if irrigated; to the left are the curious Book Mountains; in all our travel we have never seen mountains like these, looking as it were like great piles of books. At Crescent, six miles west of Thompson, is a mammoth amphitheatre formed by the walls of these cliffs, over 3,000 feet high. Now crossing the State line we enter Colorado, twisting and dodging and whirling and shying we go; now to the right is seen many

PRAIRIE DOGS,

sitting upon their little houses looking at us, and we are informed that near here there is a city of them fifteen miles square. Some twenty-five miles further on the land has been irrigated, and hundreds of cattle are grazing; frequently they get upon the track and bring the express often nearly to a standstill; here too we saw the first genuine "cowboys," with their herds of cattle and horses. Soon we arrive at Grand Junction, population 1,500, where we dine. This place is situated at the junction of Grande and Gunnison Rivers. Leaving here we run along the west bank of the Gunnison, beside high walls of rock, scant room for the train to pass, crossing little creeks, beneath overhanging cliffs, until at Delta we leave the Gunnison, as it is impossible to follow the river further so narrow grows the gorge; so we follow the Uncompahgre River valley to Montrose, the seat of Montrose Co. Here at Montrose one must change cars for Ouray, some thirty miles away, among the Rockies, named after Chief Ouray. Leaving here we begin to climb the Rockies in earnest, through snow sheds scattered here and there. Along the line we go till Cerro's summit, elevation 7,965 feet, one of the ranges, and away we go around sharp curves until Cimarron Station and the Black Canon Hotel is reached, where we once more meet the Gunnison River, following along its banks through the

BLACK CANON OF THE GUNNISON.

What shall we say; well, it was beautiful, imposing, sublime, yet awful; along this great gorge of canon the railroad lies as it were on a shelf that has been blasted out of God's wonderland. Passing Sapinero, Kezar, arriving at

GUNNISON, COLO.,

Saturday evening, March 22, the seat of Gunnison Co. The valley of the Gunnison, according to our geologists, was once a great lake, now a city is built here. Strolling through the streets we met the familiar face of an old friend, formerly of New Jersey, who kindly pointed out the places of note; one thing sure, Gunnison has an excellent hotel. Leaving Gunnison the following morning we find ourselves at the foot hills of the

GREAT MARSHALL PASS,

where we begin the ascent, our train being divided
into two sections, running up on one side of a great
canon, curving around its head, out the opposite

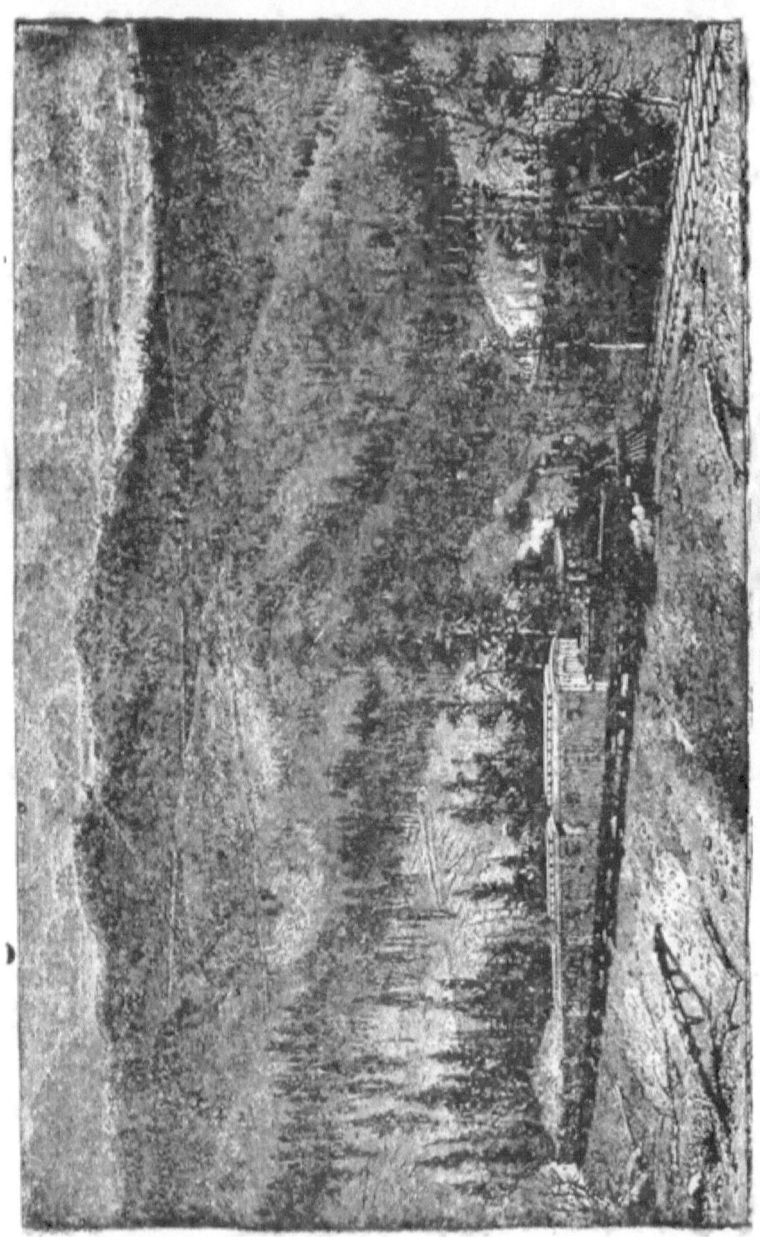

MARSHALL PASS, WESTERN SLOPE.

side, around a mountain spur, and still up another, climbing continually a grade of near 200 feet to a mile, repeating and repeating until the summit of the Marshall Pass is reached; elevation, 10,853 feet. Here the air is very light; frequently invalids expire, others faint, and nose bleed is common occurrence; we had the latter experience. Here on the north looms Mt. Ouray, elevation 14,043; beyond Mt. Antero, 14,245; Mt. Harvard,

"CASTLE GATE." (SEE PAGE 90.)

14,375, Mt. Shevano, 14,239, and many others, including Yale, Princeton, Lincoln, etc. What a lofty and magnificent sight! Of course they were covered with snow, and we stopped at the summit station under a snow shed. Now down the mountain we go, around Phantom Curve and Horse Shoe Bend, where we frequently see the other section of our train going in an opposite direction, as though they were going to California, while we were on our way to New Jersey. This great Pass must be seen to be appreciated. At last we have reached the valley of the Arkansas River, passing the noted Poncho Hot Springs on our right, fifty-five in number, and soon find that we are at Salida, Colo., situated on the west bank of the Arkansas River, an enterprising and well laid out city. Now following down the west bank of the Arkansas River we begin to enter the

GRAND CANON OF THE ARKANSAS.

As the train flies along, higher and higher become the cliffs, until 3,000 feet above the train. Are you looking for a description? Well, no mortal pen has ever described it yet, or ever can. We have twice crossed the Italian Alps, but for great rocks with high domes, towers and pinnacles, sharp corners and hollow recesses, rocks 3,000 feet high, standing perpendicular, with projective spurs almost locking from opposite sides, and just enough room for the train and river to pass; imagine these things and you will have only a faint conception of the "Royal Gorge" of the Grand Canon of the Arkansas. Leaving the Grand Canon we arrive at

CANON CITY, COLO.,

where the State Penitentiary is situated. Now leaving Canon City, at the very gate of the mountains, on to Florence we go, where oil has been discovered, giving the town a "big boom." Passing a number of small stations we arrive at

PUEBLO,

an enterprising Colorado manufacturing city, and a great railroad centre. Now turning northward we soon arrive at

COLORADO SPRINGS

on the afternoon of March 23. It is situated on a broad plateau, and is beautifully laid out, and has many fine public buildings and residences, and a population of say 20,000. But we must not leave this vicinity without seeing the

GARDEN OF THE GODS.

Early Monday morning, March 24, we are on our way by carriage, passing through the principal street of

COLORADO CITY,

population 3,000, being one of the oldest towns in Colorado. At one time the State Capital was here. On we go to

MANITOU,

a summer and winter resort, where are located sulphur, iron and soda springs, visiting the Rainbow Falls and

UTE PASS,

which is the old stage route to Leadville, and perhaps Brigham Young passed through here on his way to Utah, with his many wives; thence to the trail up by the base of

PIKE'S PEAK

we go to the Iron Springs. Returning, we enter the "Garden of the Gods," a very curious formation of the rock resembling animals, etc. Here is the postern gate, as the Grand Gateway is on the eastern side. Entering at the postern, or western gate, we have on our left the wonderful "Balanced Rock," resting its hundreds of tons upon a base hardly three feet square; close by are the Mushroom, rocks shaped precisely like great mushrooms or toad-stools, while others look like a bear,

GARDEN OF THE GODS; PIKE'S PEAK IN THE DISTANCE.

deer, camel, elephant, lion, seal, "Simese twins," "Mother Grundy," "Ben Butler," "Bride of the Gods," etc. Some of the rocks rise 330 feet. On top of one of the highest is seen a perfect stage coach and horses, with people in the coach; it certainly was a strange sight. It is supposed that these strange formations were worshiped by the Ute Indians. Now leaving Colorado Springs, passing Palmer Lake and Castle Rock, we arrive at Denver, Col., Monday evening, March 24, 1890; being 772 miles from Ogden, the Capital of Colorado, and the commercial centre. Visiting the principal streets and buildings, we must say this

Prairie City of the West is not on paper, but a reality. In 1870 the population of Denver was only 4,759; in 1880 45,629, and to-day she claims 150,000; further comments on this enterprising city are unnecessary. The Centennial State, or Colorado, area 103,925 square miles, is one of the richest States in the Union in mineral productions; and here in 1842-44 Gen. John C. Fremont made his celebrated trip across the Rocky Mountains. This State in 1870 had not one mile of railroad in use, to-day railroads are leaving Denver in almost every direction. One county in Colorado has more coal than the whole State of Pennsylvania. Saying good-bye to Denver, Wednesday, March 26, crossing the South Platte River through the prairies we go to

AKRON, COL.,

population 1,000, where we dine; 112 miles east of Denver, in the distance, are the snow-capped peaks of the Rocky Mountains. At 2.30 we cross the line near Wray, and are now in Nebraska, skirting the Republican River, "Shallow Water," as the Indians used to call it. Nebraska was organized as a territory in 1854, admitted 1867, area 76,855 square miles, population 1880, 452,402; Platte is the principal river; cattle raising is the greatest industry of the State, next to agriculture; soil said to be sixteen to twenty feet deep in Saline Co. At Culbertson, Frenchman River joins the Republican; now we are at McCook, population 3,000, electric lights, etc.; six years ago a barren prairie. Other towns along the line have a like history. On we go, and the land looks exceedingly fertile, but on the sand bluffs of Western Nebraska it is said to be very poor. Near Indianola we saw our first prairie fire, away off northward; again we see it further off at Arapahoe; arriving at

OXFORD, NEB.,

at 7.40 p.m., a town of 800, where we break our journey at a good hotel, gas, steam heat, etc.

Thursday, March 27, at 8.10 p.m., we steam out of Oxford, the next station being Orleans, branch here to St. Francis; at Republican another branch goes to Oberlin, Kansas. Still we follow the Republican River and its rich, fertile soil; now Bloomington a county seat is passed, and soon we are at Red Cloud, the home of a Nebraska cattle king owning thousands of cattle, hogs, etc., who informed us that often in Nebraska corn is used for fuel, being cheaper than coal; he supplies Leadville and Denver alone with 90 per cent. of the hogs used; also informed us that cattle, hogs and corn were the principal products of Nebraska. Now passing Amboy, where a branch runs to Hastings and Omaha, soon we reach Superior, a railroad centre; now leaving Chester we dodge in and out of Kansas four times, so close are we to the line; arriving at Waymore at 2 p.m. we dine. Soon we are at Humboldt and the country looks fine, good, healthy trees are seen, indicating of course good, rich, deep soil. Now arriving at Falls City, Nebraska, where we change cars for a

SHORT TRIP THROUGH KANSAS.

Leaving Rulo, we soon cross the State line and enter Kansas, where we follow the

MISSOURI RIVER.

Near here one sees three States, Missouri, Nebraska and Kansas, any one large enough for a kingdom or an empire.

"WHITE CLOUD,"

calls out the porter, and it's in Kansas. The

"GARDEN OF THE WEST," KANSAS,

or "Smoky Water," as the Indians used to call it, has an area of 82,080 square miles. It is the geographical centre of the United States, exclusive of Alaska, and was organized as a territor· in 1854, admitted 1861, Topeka being the capital. It is said Kansas has more corn now than railroads have cars to haul. Well, we crossed the Nemaha River, arriving at

ATCHISON, KANSAS,

Thursday afternoon, March 27; population, 25,000; a rather pretty city. Strolling up Commercial Street, then by car over Fifth and out Tenth Streets, etc., things look prosperous, but life is too short to describe all the railroad junctions, pretty little villages, towns and cities one passes, so we hasten on to the "Chicago of the West," Kansas City, and leaving Atchison early Friday morning, March 28, we crossed the great Missouri River into

MISSOURI,

the Penn. of the West, area 69,415 square miles, or nearly the combined area of the whole New England States; organized as a territory in 1812, admitted in 1821; Missouri River frontage being nearly 500 miles; now passing Sugar and Bean Lakes, where we saw thousands of wild ducks and a forest of squirrels; what a paradise for sport. Now following the east banks of the Missouri, now a distant view of Leavenworth, Kansas, flying past Grand Island, etc. Crossing the great river we hear the porter shout

KANSAS CITY, MO.,

being 654 miles from Denver, or 2,259 miles from San Francisco, where we arrive Friday morning, March 28, at 10.50 a. m. Up Independence Avenue we go all the way, then over the elevated line to Chelsea Park, Kansas City, Kansas, population 50,000, for there are two Kansas Citys. Returning now to the Missouri Kansas City, we stroll through her principal streets, then over the Twelfth Street line, passing the Exhibition Building, etc., traveling about the city some thirty miles by her splendid street car system. Well, Kansas City reminds one of San Francisco, Cal., as one sees her street cars mount the hills. Kansas City has perhaps 200,000 human beings; it is certainly a very enterprising city. Here empties the Kansas River into the Missouri. Leaving here

Saturday, March 29, at 8.25 a. m., again crossing the great river, we often see the familiar faces of the

"COLORED MAN"

or negro. Asking them a question they never fail to give you a civil answer; there are about 7,000,-000 in the United States. The race is not becoming extinct like the Maoris, but are increasing; "way down on the Swanee River," or in the Southern States they are to be found everywhere. Passing Liberty, Clay County, the early home of the famous "James boys," the notorious highwaymen, on we go to Cameron, Laclede, Bucklin, Macon, Monroe, Palmyra Junction, where one must change to go to St. Louis via this line, the principal city and commercial centre of Missouri, but as we have been there before, we hasten on to the shores of the great

MISSISSIPPI RIVER.

Now steaming up the river is seen an old-time Mississippi steamboat, with her paddle wheel behind; soon we are crossing the river on a fine steel bridge; yonder lies

QUINCY, ILL.,

reminding one of a distant view of Joppa, Palestine being similar, for both are built on a bluff. Here, too, we have a fine view of the city, and the new City Hall and Court House; population, 40,000; here we spend half an hour and dine. The area of Illinois is 56,650 square miles, and is called Prairie or Sucker State; now through Golden, Galesburg, Buda, Mendota, Aurora, on goes our express train of eleven cars, and before one is hardly aware of it the porter shouts

CHICAGO,

being 488 miles from Kansas City, where we arrived March 30, 1890. In 1801 Chicago was a swamp, 1811 a small military post, 1831 a village of twelve houses, and in 1841 an incorporated city

with 5,752 inhabitants; to-day, 1890. she claims
with her suburbs 1,200,000; we believe no city in
the world has such a record; it's one of the

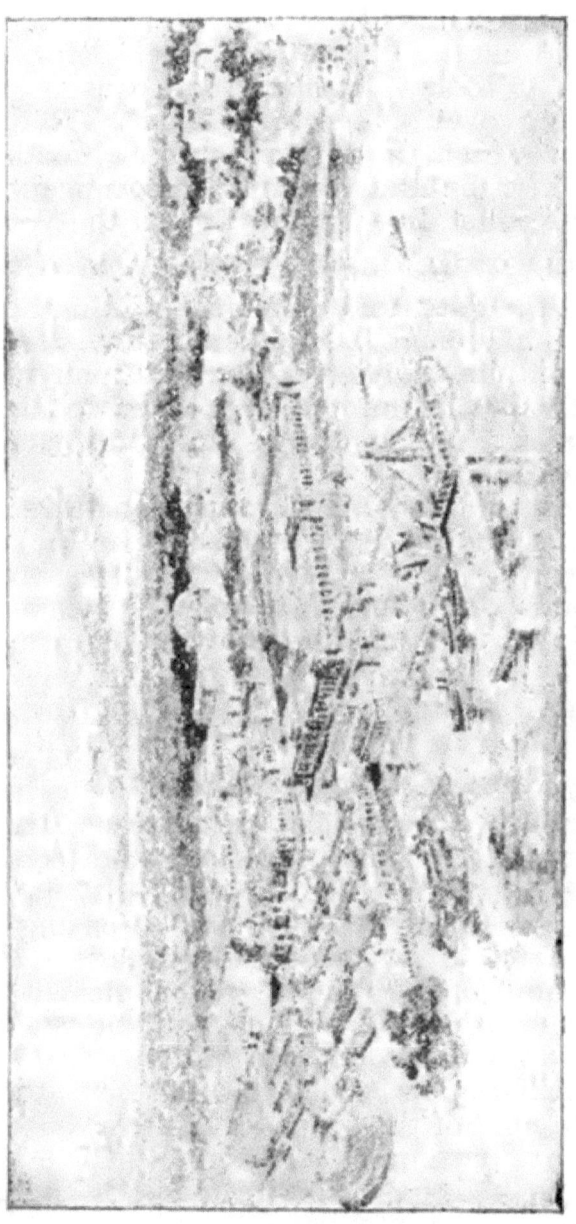

BIRD'S-EYE VIEW COLUMBIAN EXPOSITION.

greatest railroad centres in existence, the land
surrounding for hundreds of miles is exceedingly
fertile, and rainfall abundant. October 8, 1871, a
disastrous fire swept the city, but almost immediately she arose like the "phœnix" from her ashes,
building finer buildings than ever before. It is
said Mrs. O'Leary's fractious cow caused the fire,
by kicking over a kerosene lamp. To-day her
street car system is perfect; streets broad, many
shaded; her buildings simply magnificent; well
may it be called the Garden City of the West.

WORLD'S FAIR COST AND MANAGEMENT.

Before the gates of the World's Columbian Exposition shall have been opened to visitors $18,-
750,000 will have been expended upon it, inde-
pendently of the millions expended in the con-
struction of State buildings and the installation
of State exhibits.

The cost of this Exposition will be three times
as much as any previous Exposition in the history
of the world. It occupies about three times as
many acres (638), and has about twice as much
space under roof as the greatest of former Ex-
positions.

Chicago, you know, boasts of having the largest
population for its age of any city on earth; but

WHAT AFTER 2090 A. D.?

For according to the last 1890 census, the earth
is now peopled by not less than 1,468,000,000 of
human beings, and her utmost capacity is 6,000,-
000,000. The population is now increasing at the
rate of about 8 per cent. each decade. At this
rate the limit of the number of people which our
globe can comfortably support will be reached in
2090, or in about 198 years from the present time.
This calculation is based on the fact that the
habitable land of the globe amounts to only about
46,000,000 square miles, and only a little over one-
half of this, 28,000,000 square miles, is capable of
sustaining human life were the inhabitants forced

to depend on their immediate surroundings for food and raiment. The best statisticians tell us that this last 28,000,000 square miles of land is capable of maintaining 207 persons to the square mile, the whole being based on the fact that the soil of Japan now sustains 264 to the square mile and that of China 295. On and after 2090 twenty-acre farms in the Mississippi and Missouri valleys will be at a premium.

We could devote pages to this city, but the above facts speak for themselves, and after spending six days visiting the principal sights, we leave April 4. Away we go along the banks of the great Michigan Lake; on our right is seen the old exhibition building and the great Chicago Auditorium, and hundreds of pretty residences and shady streets, that extend westward as far as the eye can reach, frequently whizzing past suburban passenger trains going to and from the great city; now passing Jackson Park, to our right, one of the principal parks, soon we are at ·

MILLERS, IND.,

and we find we have left Illinois, crossing the State line, and are in Indiana or Hoosier State; area 89,350 square miles, Indianapolis being the capital and home of President Harrison. Indiana coal fields cover an area of 6,500 square miles, population 1880, 1,978,301, land rich and rainfall abundant. At Walkerton we pause to give the "iron horse" a drink, now passing through thick forests, thence out into a fine farming region, beside Syracuse Lake to Garrett at 2 p. m., being 144 miles from Chicago, where we dine. Now flying past Hicksville we find we have crossed the line and are in

OHIO,

or "Buckeye State;" area, 41,060 square miles. Cincinnati, the "Queen City" of the West, being the metropolis, and Columbus the capital, ranks first in agricultural implements, and has 247,189 farms. On we go, crossing the Mawnee River, arriving at Defiance at 3.15 p. m.; here one sees many trees and stump land, one-story frame houses, and well laid out streets. Crossing another river, passing through an oil belt at North Baltimore, where one sees a natural gas well, until Newark is reached, where one must change cars for Columbus and Cincinnati; twenty minutes for supper, cries the porter. On to Zanesville, Barnesville and Bellaire we go, where the country begins to look hilly. At Bellaire we see blazing blast furnaces, and the sight is magnificent, as we cross the

OHIO RIVER

on a fine steel bridge; arriving at Benwood the porter shouts change cars for Wheeling and Pittsburgh. Again we find we have crossed the State line and are in

WEST VIRGINIA,

or "Panhandle State;" area 34,780 square miles. Charleston being the capital and Wheeling the metropolis; here we find 39,778 farms, and iron ore yielding fifty to eighty per cent. of pure metal. Now following the banks of the Ohio, soon we turn to our left to Newburg, Deer Park, where ex-President Cleveland went to spend his "honeymoon." Over the

ALLEGHENY MOUNTAINS

we go to the summit, 2,800 feet high, now around sharp curves, soon we reach the beautiful banks of the north

POTOMAC RIVER,

arriving at Piedmont, W. Va. Crossing the river near here we are now on Maryland soil, but soon the train takes a turn as if not satisfied with Maryland, and again we are in West Virginia, these two States being separated by the Potomac; flying along the foot hills of the Allegheny, arriving at

CUMBERLAND, MD.,

at about 8 a. m., where we breakfast; now still following the banks and valley of the beautiful river, all along here now are pointed out to us scenes of skirmishing of the late war, for

"Tramp, tramp, the boys come marching."

On we go to Martinsburg, Shenandoah Junction to

HARPER'S FERRY, W. VA.,

stopping directly in front of

"JOHN BROWN'S FORT,"

a little one-story stone building; beyond lies the town, and on the very top of a hill is seen a grave-yard, where we are told the remains of "John Brown's body lies mouldering in the ground, as his soul goes marching on."

Now over a bridge we go through a gap of the

BLUE MOUNTAIN,

still following near the Potomac, and are

"ON TO WASHINGTON,"

where we arrived Saturday, April 5, 12 noon. All the way from the summit of the Allegheny to Washington the sky was and still is cloudless; winding our way to the Capitol, to the Library corridor, where we get a magnificent view of the city, thence to the Senate Chamber to visit some of our friends. Now up Pennsylvania Avenue to the White House; passing to our left is seen the great Washington monument, the highest in the world; thence out Massachusetts Avenue to greet other friends, and after visiting the principal sights, away to the station we go and soon find ourselves in

BALTIMORE, MARYLAND,

as the train speeds along at the rate of a mile a minute. Up Howard Street to Lombard, Sharp, German, Baltimore and Charles Streets, to Mt. Vernon Place. Here one sees Walters' famous picture gallery, perhaps one of the finest private collections in the world; near by here is the house of Robert Garrett, the millionaire railroad king, whose house resembles Vanderbilt's in New York. Here also is a fine monument to the "Father of

THE CAPITOL, WASHINGTON, D. C.

Our Country," but time flies, and we must wend our way back to the vestibuled express train, and soon find ourselves flying along the western shore of Maryland at the rate of a mile a minute. One of the thirteen original States is Maryland, and named in honor of Maria, wife of Charles II., King of England; area 12,210 square miles. At Havre de Grace we cross the

SUSQUEHANNA RIVER.

To our left is Port Deposit, and soon we find that we have arrived at

NEWARK, DEL.,

another of the original thirteen States; area 2,050 square miles. Now to Wilmington and on to Chester, where we find we have again crossed the line into

PENNSYLVANIA,

or "Keystone State," named in honor of William Penn; area 45,215 square miles. On we go to

PHILADELPHIA,

and soon are comfortably situated in a first-class hotel, where we have arrived Saturday, April 5, at 7.30 p. m.; population is said to exceed one million, and covering more ground than any other one city, as the people as a rule live in their own homes. We are told 15,000 new houses are to be built this year. Here, in 1876, President U. S. Grant turned the wheel and set in motion one of the greatest "Centennial Exhibitions" known up to that time. Here, in 1776, was signed the Declaration of Independence. Directly opposite, over the Delaware River, lies Camden, New Jersey, and beyond, eastward some thirty miles, is the shore of the Atlantic Ocean and Atlantic City; further south Cape May; beautiful summer resorts, where Philadelphia people go to spend their vacation. Wednesday, April 9, at one o'clock, we leave the great

QUAKER CITY,

under the Girard Avenue bridge we go; to our left and right is seen Fairmount Park; as we run along the shores of the Schuylkill River, in the distance one catches a glimpse of some of the old Centennial buildings, along side of Laurel Hill, to Wayne Junction, on, on we go and soon find that we are

"CROSSING THE DELAWARE,"

not as Gen. Washington did near here, over one hundred years ago, but on a magnificent steel bridge, on to Trenton Junction, Bound Brook, Plainfield, Elizabeth, to our left now is seen the distant smoke from the busy manufacturing city of Newark, New Jersey. Soon we are crossing Newark Bay, on a bridge some three miles long, to Bergen Point; now to our right is seen the Bartholdi Statue of Liberty, and a distant view of New York City, Brooklyn and Brooklyn Bridge, before us lies the great New York Harbor and Bay.

"JERSEY CITY,

all change," cries the porter, for here one must take the ferry going to New York. New Jersey, or "Jersey Blue," is named in honor of Sir George Carteret, at one time Governor of the Island of Jersey, England; it is one of the thirteen original States, area 7,815 square miles, extreme length 157 miles, width thirty-seven to seventy, lying between two of the largest cities in either North or South America, Newark being the metropolis while Trenton is the capital. Now crossing the beautiful Hudson River, the River Rhine of America, on the ferryboat Communipaw, arriving at New York City Wednesday evening, April 9, 1890; a city, including its suburbs, of some 3,000,-000 human beings, for what else are Brooklyn, Jersey City, Newark, etc., but suburbs, counting as London, England, does, including her many suburbs. New York, the Empire or Excelsior State, is one of the original thirteen; area 49,170 square miles, New York City being the metropolis and Albany the capital. To describe this great city and suburbs would fill a volume, so we will not attempt it.

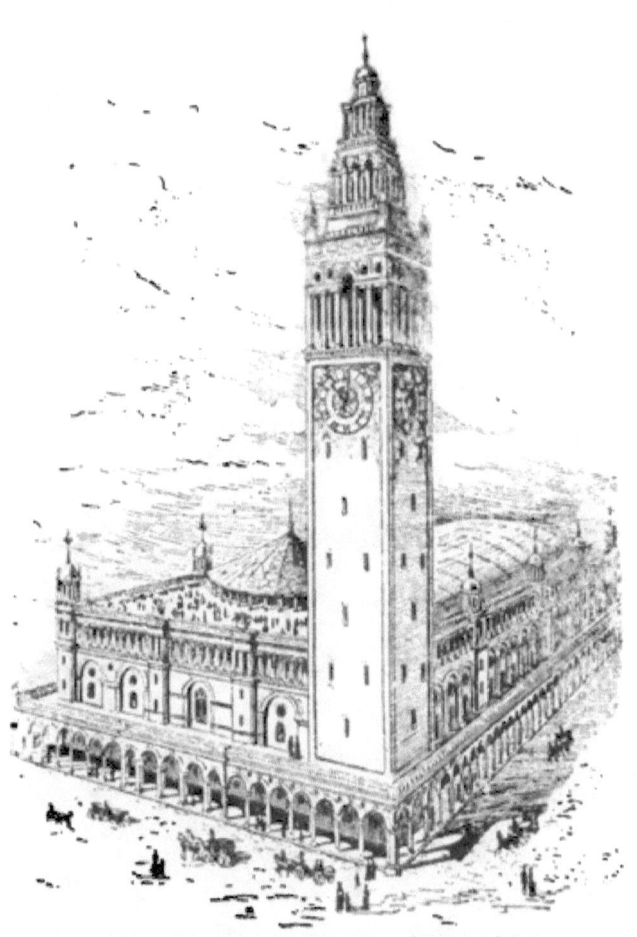

MADISON SQUARE GARDEN, NEW YORK CITY.

STATUE OF LIBERTY, BROOKLYN BRIDGE IN THE DISTANCE.

Down the New York Bay we get a glimpse of the Statue of Liberty, a gift from France. Over the Hoboken Ferry we go to Hoboken, Paterson,

Boonton, Dover, Hackettstown; whizzing through Port Murray, to our left is seen Mt. Lebanon and the

OLD HOMESTEAD,

our birth place; soon we have arrived at Washington, Warren County, New Jersey, United States of America. Down Railroad Avenue we go, up Broad Street to the

BEATTY BUILDING,

(The Beatty Building.)

having completed our tour of the world in 166 days, leaving here October 25, 1889, and arriving home April 9, 1890; being 71 miles from New York or one thousand one hundred and eleven miles from Chicago via Harper's Ferry, or thirty-five thousand nine hundred and seventy-four miles since June, 1889 (see preface). Having now visited many nations, seen some wonderful and very curious sights, especially in Palestine (Holy Land) and Egypt, looked upon the faces of many human beings of different tongues and religious beliefs; of the over fourteen (14) hundred millions of human beings now living upon the face of the earth at the present time, (1890 census), we have learned a lesson, that there are other great nations as, well as the United States of America.

THE END.